GERT LEDIG

The
Stalin Organ

Translated with an introduction by
MICHAEL HOFMANN

Granta Books
London

Granta Publications, 2/3 Hanover Yard, Noel Road, London N1 8BE

First published in Great Britain by Granta Books 2004
First published in Germany as *Die Stalinorgel* in 1955

A CIP catalogue record for this book is available from the British Library.

1 3 5 7 9 10 8 6 4 2

Typeset by M Rules
Printed and bound in Great Britain
by Bookmarque Ltd, Croydon, Surrey

INTRODUCTION

Payback, translated by Shaun Whiteside and published by Granta in 2003, was Gert Ledig's second novel. It is a brutally horrible account of seventy minutes – a 'bomber's hour' – over an unnamed German city in 1944. As well as by the unstinting capacity to imagine and depict horror (and in particular a gruesome resourcefulness in chronicling some of the more extreme varieties of violent death), Ledig distinguishes himself by devising an impressively original vertical vision for the book, which literally makes a showing on every level: from the relative serenity of the American bomber crew, torn between vindictiveness and compassion (not that it matters much, they are one of four hundred); to the teenage ack-ack gunners on a tower four floors up; to a hapless old couple with nothing left to live for following the death of their son, looking at least to die together in their own home; to the lawlessness of street level, with bullying gangs of soldiers running rampant; to the underground shelter, finally, where desperate civilians sit out what may at any time turn out to be their last moments in darkness and fear. The two – downwardly – mobile things in a deliberately, stiflingly claustrophobic book are the American bombs, and Sergeant Strenehen, the American gunner, who accidentally follows them to their target area.

Ledig's first book, originally published in 1955, the year before *Payback*, was *The Stalin Organ*. A Stalin organ is (I think) a reasonably current term of military slang for a multiple rocket launcher; the bunch of rockets does indeed look like organ pipes, or cigarettes in a packet; at the time, I would guess they were as destructive as anything conventional and terrestrial that had been invented. (The word isn't used anywhere in the book, but the weapon's effects are described in the Runner's second scenario, on page 14). The setting here is outside Leningrad in the summer of 1942, some time after Hitler broke his pact with Stalin and prepared the way for some of the most tenaciously horrible fighting in the whole of the Second World War. (Ledig fought here, just as, incidentally, he had been a civilian later – it was in Munich – to witness the bombing of the cities.) Once again, the reader will sup full of horrors; but these things happened, are presently happening, and presumably will continue to happen; there is no point in pretending otherwise, and neither honour or security in putting them beyond the reach of literature. Not every writer wants, or is able to write about them, but in this bleak and daunting specialism, Gert Ledig is certainly a writer who should be read. In the brief spell of his life that he gave to writing, he wrote about nothing else. In an almost Faustian way, one might think he kept his side of the bargain. Each of his three books is a 'war book'.

In the time since I first read Ledig, two years ago, I have revised my opinion of him as a writer. Nothing finds out a writer like translating him, and Ledig, I am glad to say, comes out of it, in my view, as someone of considerable skill and reach. It is easy to think of him – as the German critics have done, to some extent – as a necessary purveyor of unpleasantnesses, but he is better than that. He is a dramatic novelist, who works in scenes and writes clever dialogue. He organizes war into a plot, and drives its full force through what – among so much intentional mayhem and blind chance – come to seem relatively fine capillaries, like individual psychology and cause and effect. A whole chain of intrigue is set in motion by slight impairments of judgement and hairline reactions to events. *The Stalin Organ* is a thoroughly worked out, plotted book. War, for all its random destructiveness, is proposed to us as a machine, and the novel is also a machine. There is the intricacy almost of farce in its operation. (Think about the episode near the end, say, where the Sergeant has to be killed, as it were for bureaucratic or accounting reasons, because he is already dead on paper.) It hits you with the Whitehall farce and the Imperial War Museum, both together. It is an unlikely thing in a book in which ranks are used in preference to names (and I have therefore capitalized them, to make them stand out a little better), but we actually come to understand a great deal about individual motivation of the different characters. In a way, the whole idea of 'character' in relation to war is preposterous – especially as much of the character shown is so petty or malignant – but on the other hand, it's all there is, and it may make the difference between living and dying. Character, as the Greeks knew, is destiny. All this is used by Ledig to make not just a picture, but actually a moral vision of war, not least as something psychologically deforming.

The Stalin Organ is, among other things, a sort of riposte to Ernst Jünger, whose 1920 book, *Storm of Steel*, glorified the violence of World War One, and asserted both the value of war and the triumph of the human spirit. The trench fighting (unexpected in the Second World War) and the military landscape both seem to me to hark back to World War One; the syllable 'stal' appears in both titles; there is one explicit reference to Jünger's book on page 82 ('A black steel storm hung menacingly over the Front.'). Having, quite fortuitously, translated both books in the space of little over a year, it wasn't just my fault that I sometimes didn't know where I was! While Ledig's account of warfare – most unlike Jünger's – sticks rigorously and programmatically to its 'low', discreditable aspects, such things as suicide, murder, self-mutilation, desertion and dementia – it also, very occasionally, offers strikingly aestheticizing touches, much as Jünger does. 'thin strokes of a barbed wire fence' (page 59) is a phrase of Japanese pen-and-ink *delicatesse* with black and white; and one bizarre phrase on page 149, about 'red and green pansy-coloured pearls' (*penseefarben* – it's quite as odd as that in German) must be a take-off of Jünger's celebrated or notorious sense of colour. Ledig described *The Stalin Organ* as '*eine Kampfschrift*', which is the German word for pamphlet or polemic; he might have written it specifically against Jünger, who might have called his own book exactly the same thing – only in its literal sense of 'fighting writing'.

Like *Payback*, *The Stalin Organ* is a strikingly geometrical book. Where that had its vertical strata of activity, in keeping with the thrust of the bombing war, *The Stalin Organ* sticks pretty much to one plane in its choice of terrain – the railway line, a few roads, woods and swamps, and above all the hill – but contrives a situation in which each side is surrounded. (It is characteristic of Ledig that he treats both sides equally; he

is almost democratically impartial in his treatment.) Both the
Major's desperate band of Germans and Trupikov's Russians
are encircled. The pattern reminds me of the circles in a man-
dala, with each set in a preponderance of the other. Or
perhaps of the Ugolino episode in Dante's *Inferno*, where both
Ugolino and his opponent, Archbishop Roger, are bitten fast
into the other. Against that greater symmetry, there are
numerous other instances of symmetry or parity of detail: the
woundings and killings, the journeys, the glimmerings of
another, civilian life, occasional italic inserts for flashbacks or
hallucinations, down to quite tiny things like rings, diagrams,
cigarettes and pieces of paper. This strongly symmetrical
structuring allows each actor in the interdependent drama to
function as a possible centre, the hero of his or her own story:
the Runner, the Captain, the Major, Zostchenko, Sonia,
Trupikov, the Sergeant. The contrast with, as it were, the
standard 'war story', with its single sanctioned point of iden-
tification and single line of action, could not be stronger than
with Ledig's mobile sympathies and versatile changes of angle.

Perhaps the thing that for me clinches Ledig's quality as a
writer is what he does with nothing. (It's like looking at the
lower edge of religious or otherwise heroic Renaissance paint-
ings, at the sampler of stray plants and insects one often finds.)
One would have to concede, I think, that his writing about the
extremities of life and action – say, pain, danger, cruelty – is
persuasive, and that Ledig's trademark way of registering
insults to dead bodies is unforgettably macabre, but what is he
like without such things? I would see it in a detail such as the
moth he has fluttering around the lamp while the Cavalry
Captain is being interrogated, or the spider's web he feels in his
face in the barn, shortly after. I would point to a sentence – a

courtly, lacquered, Japanese sentence – like: 'A beetle in shining armour dragged a blade of grass across the path' (page 13), in the middle of all sorts of dread and drama. (Quite possibly, incidentally, another Jünger touch, for Jünger was a noted entomologist.) Or, in the same scene: 'There was a field-kitchen installed on the edge of the forest. The co-driver was feeding fresh wood into the furnace. A few embers spilled out. The lid of the cauldron was open. The steam smelled of nothing in particular.' (page 32) That 'nothing in particular' – a lesser writer would have given you God knows what – is actually a touch of greatness. It's the same thing, I think, later on in the book, where Shalyeva, after her ordeal as a nurse, notices the softness of the grass; or where the Runner, after pages of the most brutal torture, and after picking up his teeth (the description 'hard pieces of dirt with blood on them' is unforgettable), is given this simple sentence: 'He ran in the sun.'

When *The Stalin Organ* first appeared in 1955, having been rejected by fifty publishers, it surprised pretty much everyone by being a considerable success. It sold many copies, and was translated into several other languages. Then it disappeared, its successors disappeared, and Ledig himself disappeared. For a variety of reasons, he wasn't cut out for a literary career, and the divided Germany of the 1950s wasn't perhaps the place to offer one to the likes of him either. By the time he died in 1999, he knew – ironically! – that there was a Ledig revival on the way, but he didn't live to see any of his books in print again.

Michael Hofmann
New Brunswick
October 2003

PROLOGUE

The Lance-Corporal couldn't turn in his grave, because he didn't have one. Some three versts from Podrova, forty versts south of Leningrad, he had been caught in a salvo of rockets, been thrown up in the air, and with severed hands and head dangling, been impaled on the skeletal branches of what once had been a tree.

The NCO, who was writhing on the ground with a piece of shrapnel in his belly, had no idea what was keeping his machine-gunner. It didn't occur to him to look up. He had his hands full with himself.

The two remaining members of the unit ran off, without bothering about their NCO. If someone had later told them they should have made an effort to fetch the Lance-Corporal down from his tree, they would quite rightly have said he had a screw loose. The Lance-Corporal was already dead, thank God. Half an hour later, when the crippled tree trunk was taken off an inch or two above the ground by a burst of machine-gun fire, his wrecked body came down anyway. In the intervening time, he had also lost a foot. The frayed sleeves of his tunic were oily with blood. By the time he hit the ground, he was just half a man.

With the machine gun out of action, the log-road lay open before Lieutenant Vyacheslav Dotoyev's shock troops. He motioned to the rumbling tank in front of what was left of his little bunch of art students from the Stalin Academy. The chains rattled. Another minute, and what was left of the Lance-Corporal was rolled flat. The budding artists didn't even get a chance to go through his pockets.

Once the tank-tracks had rolled out the Lance-Corporal, a fighter plane loosed off its explosive cannonfire into the mass of shredded uniform, flesh and blood.

After that, the Lance-Corporal was left in peace.

For four weeks, he gave off a sweetish smell. Till only his bones were left on the grassy forest floor. He never got a grave. A couple of days after he lost his hands, his Captain set his name to a report. The Sergeant had drawn it up.

Quite a few of these reports had come in. The Captain on that day signed seven, but the Sergeant showed no sign of flagging. The reports were submitted in order of rank. The report on the decease of the Lance-Corporal was signed after the report on the NCO. In this way, the Sergeant kept a little order. These and other such refinements meant he was indispensable at headquarters. He didn't realize he was simultaneously taking orders from fate. Only the Lance-Corporal would have been in a position to confirm that the beginning of the salvo had hit his NCO, and that it wasn't for another second or two that he himself was hurled into the air. But the Lance-Corporal was in no condition to give a report. He didn't even have a hand with which to salute. And so there was a touch of providence in the way everything was taken care of.

When the Captain signed the reports now, he no longer bothered to ask the Sergeant whether such and such a man was married or not, or whether his mother was still alive. By the time his own turn came, no one would bother either. Asking such a question didn't exactly do him any good. It wasn't that he cared. He wanted to live, they all wanted to live. He had reached the conclusion that it was better just to stay alive, and forget about playing the hero.

When he got the chance – which happened most nights – he would try to make a deal with God, after ten years in which he hadn't given Him a thought. Depending on the intensity of the bombardment that was coming down on the shelter, he would offer Him a hand, or a foot. In return for letting him live. When the Russians took the log-road, he offered God both his feet. It was only his eyes that he wouldn't give up. He didn't mention them in his prayers.

So far, however, God hadn't shown much interest in doing a deal. Maybe it was His way of taking revenge for the ten years in which he hadn't thought about Him? It was a difficult thing for the Captain to renew their relationship after such a long time. To begin a conversation with God as if he were still a deputy headmaster seemed ridiculous under the present circumstances. Better, then, to step before Him as a company commander. But that made it harder to dicker over his personal fate. The Captain left his request till the very end of his prayer. His only way of making its importance clear was by declaring his readiness to take certain sacrifices upon himself. It wasn't until later that it occurred to him to implore God humbly for his life. Later, when he was forced to stay in his shelter and wait while a Russian outside decided whether or not to toss in a hand-grenade. After ten years as a deputy headmaster, he couldn't know that you didn't need God for the fulfilment of such a prayer.

A Corporal, who hadn't given God a thought, had scratched at the soil with his bare hands for so long that the skin on his fingertips hung down in shreds, and then he had calmly sat and watched as flies and mosquitoes had settled on the raw flesh and introduced into his organism certain substances that he required for the fulfilment of his plan. A few days later, with swollen hands, a high temperature, and various other ambiguous symptoms, he had been taken to the dressing-station. That Corporal had taken the easy way. He hadn't tormented himself with any relationship to God. It was twenty years since he had last seen inside a church. Later on, he felt no desire to, and God didn't cross his path a second time.

But these were matters that were only loosely bound up with the report on the Lance-Corporal's going missing in action. More directly concerned with it was the Runner at company command-post. He stuffed the piece of paper in his pocket along with his pipe and the last of some sunflower seeds he had taken off a Russian prisoner. He was never given very long to spend at operational command.

The road to battalion headquarters was neither a road nor did it offer any sort of security. Several times a day the Runner ran for his life on a sort of cross-country track. This race against death he principally owed to the Sergeant, who kept up a never-ending stream of important communications to the battalion, to justify his continued presence in the company bunker. He needed to make his case several times a day, lest it occur to the Captain to give him the command of a platoon in the front line. That it was only a matter of time till the Runner's two children became orphans was no concern of the Sergeant's.

The Runner was most afraid of the first hundred yards outside the command-post. A Russian mortar had got the range of the company bunker. It regularly scattered its splinters over the little parapet. No one who was hit and lay there for longer than a second ever lived. The Russian marksmen shot at every unmoving target. As the Runner and the Sergeant both knew.

Each time the Runner went out on one of these pointless missions, he resolved to pay the Sergeant back. He wouldn't have been capable of killing an enemy in cold blood, but the next time they were under attack he would shoot the Sergeant in the back. He hated him. The heart was half a hand's breadth beneath the shoulderblade. He had to know some anatomy for his job. He was proud of it. Each time he ran those critical hundred yards, he had murder on his mind. Then came the bushes, and he was over the worst. If he got caught up in some machine-gun fire there, that was just bad luck.

The road only got truly hopeless when it went across the bluff. Up there, it looked like a lunar landscape. Only you wouldn't have come across a huge steel pylon on the moon. A few of its props and struts stuck out, warped by direct hits. But the mighty concrete root of it withstood any calibre. Not far from the pylon was a soldier's tomb. It probably dated from the early days of the advance. A low birch fence surrounded the mound. The cross bearing the name had been smashed by a shell. Within the company, it was referred to as 'the grave of the unknown soldier'.

The hill with the pylon on it would have served as an ideal observation point for the whole sector, except that setting up a periscope on the ploughed earth would have been rather like putting a mirror in a cement mixer.

While the Runner was flitting like a ghost across the heights, he was in another world. Gravity seemed to have been suspended. He flew rather than ran past the sputtering shells. Any thought was a waste of time. A cold wind howled across the bare expanse. The spirit kingdom had taken him in. The horsemen of the Apocalypse were giving chase. Death in the van, on his bony nag. Not a tree, not a bush, not a blade of grass. Only scuffed, sandy soil. In the craters occasional murky puddles.

And even so, there were men up here. A Corporal and a couple of Privates. One night, they had dug themselves a hole under the concrete with their bare hands and a short field-shovel. And there they stayed, biding their time till their company down in the trenches was finally wiped out. Then, they had to rush out with their explosive charges to meet the approaching steel monsters, and, with their bodies already shot to pieces, hang the magnetic charges on the tanks as they ground past. That was the moment they were waiting for, hour by hour, day after day. Always in the hope that it might never come. The lump of concrete over their heads creaked and quaked. Sand dribbled down the sides of their dugout. If the tanks didn't come, the alternative was the moment that the concrete mass settled on top of them. The percussive force of the shells made the dugout ever larger. With every day it became more apparent: the concrete pediment that supported the weight of the pylon would one day squash the little air-pocket beneath it. And in spite of that, they couldn't leave. What, to go and lie in a shellhole, and die within the hour?

The Corporal and his two men were living as in a prison. They lay side by side. In amongst their stinking bodies were containers full of dynamite. From battered mugs they drank a black liquid that purported to be coffee, dyed water that tasted of metal and chicory. On their tongues they felt the gritty sand that incessantly rained down from the ceiling into their drinking vessels. From time to time they got undressed, and went crawling around their hole like naked hermits, looking for small, greasy-looking vermin in their uniforms. Every day they waited avidly for the bottle of alcohol that they were allotted. They emptied it in next to no time, and every day they felt more astonished by their own unchanged sobriety. When they defecated, they did so either on the field-shovel, or else in empty tin cans. Then they would shovel it outside. That way, they didn't have to risk their lives. Sometimes the shit would come sliding back in. They were like lemurs. The hair grew down over their collars. They were simultaneously dusty and greasy. But always – whether eating, sleeping, smoking or drinking – they kept their ears pricked for a certain sound, and tried to set aside the howl of shells. They were waiting for the clatter of approaching Russian tanks.

Several times a day, less often at nighttime, the Runner would visit them in their hole. He was their go-between with the world, which for them had shrunk to a mile or so of Front. Every word of his that bore any relation to 'relief' would be repeated and chewed over for hours, even days, to come. And the days went by. In the forgotten army, the anti-tank unit was a zero.

They would shake hands with every man whom the Runner brought along to reinforce the Front, and secretly pray for his death, because he strengthened the company's fighting force, and reduced their chances of being relieved.

They dug around quite unabashed in the Runner's leather satchel, and in the half-light, spelled out the notifications of deaths with grim satisfaction. They could work out exactly when the company would be reduced to a mere handful of men, and its withdrawal from the Front would have purely symbolic significance. That was all that interested them in the Runner's satchel. The situation report that he carried from battalion headquarters to the company every day wasn't worth their attention. The performance report that the Sergeant had composed for divisional staff on the new machine gun drew a pitying smile from them. The Corporal used it to light his pipe with. In this way, he prevented a certain officer at battalion HQ from being reminded of the Sergeant's existence.

The Corporal functioned as an unofficial censor of the Sergeant's communications with the back area. He saw to it that the man didn't get above himself. A letter from the Sergeant to the Major disappeared without trace in the black hole of the Anti-Tank Unit. The Sergeant's name was on a list of those eligible for leave. By the time the list reached headquarters, his name was crossed out. 'Temporarily irreplaceable,' the Corporal had written next to it. Just as it's only a short step from the dramatic to the comic, so in that lousy shithole under the hill of death, Prank and Terror were cheek by jowl.

The Runner left the hole. Before he turned away, he said without emphasis that – if he was still alive – he would look in on them on the way back. His remark was superfluous. His overstrained lungs would have forced him to stop at the hole in any case. He was just talking to keep his courage up. In fact, he might as well have said a prayer.

Once more, he scuttled across the pockmarked landscape. Armour-piercing shells twittered round him like sparrows. A geyser of earth from a shell impact swallowed him up and spat him out again. In his fingers he clutched his satchel. He dashed over craters and through trenches, and finished up, shaking like a malaria sufferer, behind the rail embankment. Even though he was now back in the front line, the embankment did offer a certain protection. Shells arced across the sky like fireworks. From horizon to horizon. Not one left its trajectory. He could hear rifle fire, but it didn't scare him. The rails seemed to constitute a border of sorts. Only the splashing mortar rounds forced him to continue at his brisk pace. Even here, he wasn't safe from a chance hit. The only advantage of these five hundred yards along the rails was that they temporarily took away the solitariness that made the fear just a little harder to bear. Every fifty yards, a mud-encrusted figure would be leaning against the embankment. Even though these figures kept their eyes front the whole time, and hardly ever turned to look at him, their mere being there had something soothing about it.

His mistaken feeling of security lasted till he reached the vicinity of the dressing-station. The sight of the rigid corpses next to the path shattered all his illusions. He started off with those who had been brought there half bled to death, or with severed limbs.

The bearers were sorry to see that the burden they were transporting on their canvas was already dead. They yanked the birch pole out of the tube that was sewn together from two canvas sheets. They slid the body out, and left it lying by the dressing-station. Continual fire restricted their missions to nighttime, and for them the night ended when day started to grey. They were in a hurry, because they had to lug munitions or soggy bread up to the Front, in the same canvas.

The Runner saw the dead lying there. Those who were shot in the belly writhed in agony till the moment of death. If he couldn't pick them out by their curled-up bodies, then by their bared bellies. They could be classed as hopeless. Their removal was nothing but a courtesy they couldn't be refused as long as their brains were still functioning. Or again their screaming made it imperative. It all depended on circumstances. And circumstances varied.

For example, the railway line was back in use a couple of miles away. The front line – or what was marked as the front line on the general staff maps – wasn't always identical with the railway. The rails headed off in an easterly direction. At the point where it was out of range of the medium German batteries, the Russians used it in their logistical system. One platoon had been assigned the task of disrupting this system by blowing up the tracks, before the company took up position in advance of the height. The platoon was led by a Lieutenant (this was just eight weeks ago). He and his men were of the view that this was more properly a job for the airforce. The Sergeant, on the other hand, maintained that such decisions could only be taken higher up; he had complete confidence in the planning of this strategically important undertaking. He would always talk like that when putting together units, and usually he would end up by saying he regretted his commitments didn't permit him to take part in whatever undertaking it was. Only Engineer

Meller dared look the Sergeant sardonically in the eye as he said it. Regularly he would ask him with an expressionless face to come along anyway, and these invitations were a reason why Engineer Meller had been repeatedly passed over for promotion. It wasn't until Meller was no longer among the living that the Sergeant could find it in himself to say a gracious word about him. After the dynamiting of the railway tracks had been successfully carried out eight miles behind the Russian lines, Engineer Meller got a shot in the belly. The bullet caught him from behind, just left of the spine, and an inch below the belt. It passed through his body, and exited just left of his navel. No one in the platoon had time even to look at the wound. It was just that Engineer Meller had a scorched hole at the front and back of his tunic, which meant he was unable to carry on as a stretcher-bearer for the dead Lieutenant. The NCO had to make a split-second decision whether to abandon the Lieutenant's body or take it. He didn't need a further second in which to decide whether to dump the superfluous munitions boxes to get another man to carry the Engineer. The Engineer said he could still walk. A couple of hundred yards further on, the munitions boxes and their carrier fell by the wayside anyway: the man had got himself blown up by an anti-personnel mine. Two more men were wounded in the same incident, and the situation became critical. The Corporal fired off his remaining bullets, then he dumped his gun and accessories in a puddle. Meller was starting to lag, and the NCO was compelled to stay behind with him. Turning round, he loosed off a few clips from his submachine gun into the line of brown snipers behind him. Only the beginning of the marshes saved the group from further losses. They disappeared into the underbrush. Now they had to find the path that had slipped them right through the Russian advance guard. Within half an hour, the Corporal had found it. All this time, Engineer Meller kept insisting

he could walk unaided. They had made another half a mile or so
through the swamp when the Corporal saw an enemy machine gun
up ahead on the path. So the unit was surrounded. With a pained
half-smile on his face, Meller volunteered to take care of it. A nod
from the NCO gave him permission to run at the surprised
machine-gun crew with a couple of live hand-grenades. When the
remaining six men of the detachment leapt up from their cover after
the explosion, they ran straight past the dying Engineer. He was
lying on his back, cut off at the thigh by a machine-gun burst. It
was possible he was still alive at the point that a Russian, furious at
the shredding of his comrades, had rammed a bayonet into his chest.
Only the Runner saw the NCO level his pistol at the Engineer's
head. The sight of the NCO, unconcerned with his own safety,
calmly saluting the dead man, was something the Runner would
never forget, and nor did he ever speak about what he had seen.
He didn't have the words for it. But he was the only one to under-
stand why the NCO was unable to write the letter to Frau Meller
(the one with the standard references in it to 'shot in the chest' and
'painless death'). The Sergeant had to take care of that for him.

So even with belly shots, it depended on circumstances. The
bulk of the corpses were recruited from those who had died of
various wounds. One stretched his arms and legs up into the
air. Another lay naked on the grass, his skin chargrilled by a
flame-thrower. The Runner could have spent an hour just
looking at them all.

But already he was approaching the dressing-station. This
was where the dead and the living parted company. It was
more than he could do to look at this inferno of a charnel-
house. He passed it with eyes tight shut. But in his ears he
heard the groans and cries, and the whimpering for water.

After that, he turned off left into the wood. The trees – or what was left of them – seemed to swallow him up. They offered protection against mortars, sniper fire and shrapnels. The whistling in the air overhead only began to matter again once he reached the artillery positions.

As soon as he entered the wood, he felt alone. The brush, the birch trunks – everything was silent. The log-road, built by Russian soldiers who had long since died of starvation or been shot, swayed silently underfoot. A swarm of mosquitoes danced over a dead body in the murky puddle in the clearing. A beetle in shining armour dragged a blade of grass across the path. A ring of scorched grass, an uprooted tree and a pile of broken boughs indicated that death had been at work, days previously, just yesterday, or even a matter of hours ago. A few sunbeams managed to break through the leaves and reach the ground. The air shook. A white scrap of wool dangling from a twig warned those in the know of the presence of a minefield. Behind the Runner, there was a rumble like a parting thunderstorm. He was all alone. Loneliness constricted his heart. He sensed an ambush. There were two possibilities. One was as silent as the wood itself. It gave no notice. It lay hidden behind a tree or in the tall grass. It would come out of the bushes like a sudden whiplash. The blow was always fatal, but at least it was quick. This possibility was equipped with a pistol and a bundle of rags. Half-starved, ground down by the same fear as he was himself, it lurked behind a tree. A lightning flash and a whiplash. Maybe a little puff of smoke as well. Then a silent brown shape would leap out from its covert. Bend over the dead body. Prise the weapon out of its hands. Burrow frantically through its pockets. Valuables and junk disappeared among the rags. And it was all over in a trice. All that was left was a dead man that the mosquitoes danced over, till someone one day found him. If it was marshy, then he wouldn't be found.

The other possibility had a similar outcome. Only you were given warning. You heard animal roaring in the distance. A dull groan, a sound like nothing else. It was like a shout that could be heard over miles. Two or three times you heard it. Then the wailing of an out-of-tune organpipe. An entire sector of the Front suffered paralysis. The ticking of machine guns broke off. The snipers pulled in their rifles. The mortar crews moved closer together. The order to fire died on the lips of the artillerymen. Even the Runner cut his stride. And then it came. Innumerable lightnings ripped into the forest. Almost half a hundred shells exploded against trees or on the ground. A deafening uproar. Fire, dynamite fumes, lumps of brass as big as your fist, earth, dust. An entire artillery unit, with four guns, stacks of ammunition crates, cartridges, equipment and horses, wallowed on the ground. An hour later, the field-kitchen copped it. Driver, co-driver, cook, cold rations for sixty men and a hundred litres of watery soup were vaporized. A few minutes after that, it visited a company that was marching towards the Front on relief: eighty men, with difficulty pepped up behind the lines for a week, polished boots, oiled weapons. The forty who made it to the trenches were filthy, bloodied, demoralized. In the space of two hours, two days, two weeks. Somewhere a tank brigade was advancing into position. In the security of a hollow the commander assembled his tank crews for a final discussion. A noise on the horizon. Five or six seconds of oppressive silence. Shells burst out of nowhere. Screams. Rubble raining down on empty tanks. The youngest officer had trouble getting together enough drivers to move the dozen tanks and their dead crews back. And all who felt the shaking of the earth and saw the smoke of the explosions going up into the sky thanked (depending on their belief) fate or God that someone else had been hit, and they had got lucky this time. The Runner, too, who had gone down on his knees and covered his face with his hands thanked his destiny. And that was the second possibility.

The Runner carried on along the log-road, reports and sunflower seeds in his pocket. He wasn't even halfway, this wasn't the time to stop off anywhere. The wailing over the trees got louder. He had reached the beginning of the artillery emplacements. The forest thinned out. There was the odd clearing with thick underbrush and poisonous mushrooms. The log-road came to an end here. A motor track began that turned into thick gloop when it rained. A smashed wagon by the roadside. Mouldering leather harness and the bones of a horse. Either side of the track, cardboard signs posting mysterious instructions, signifying that the telephone exchange for a howitzer battery was situated here, or that there in the clearing, almost underground, an ack-ack gun stretched its overlong barrel up into the air. At another place, crude death's heads warned of mines.

Suddenly something came gurgling down from the sky. The Runner threw himself flat. The explosion washed over him. An enormous net that he had taken for a pile of dry brushwood flipped up along with masses of foliage. In a pile of dust stood the barrel of a gun concealed under the netting. For an instant it was dead straight. Then it crumpled. Someone who hadn't been hit cursed God. Someone else called for an ambulanceman.

The Runner got to his feet, padded on. He thought: the

call for an ambulanceman isn't something you hear that much of. The track widened, the groove worn by tyres got deeper. A soldier approached. Leather satchel, dusty boots, wizened face with sunken eyes: a Runner coming back to hell after being safe somewhere for a couple of hours. A nod, a tired smile by way of reply. And on.

The Runner quickened his step to catch up with a cart that was grinding along ahead of him. The cart was lurching about on the ploughed track. The cloud of dust it drew behind it wrapped itself round the Runner like a veil. He felt a furry taste on his tongue. The back of the cart was sheeted in canvas. A scrawny horse was between the traces. It wasn't until the Runner reached up to pull himself on board that he saw what the cart was carrying. Under the tarpaulin, stiff hands were pounding on the crusted boards, and bare heads were nodding up and down. The passengers prodded stiff legs into each other's bellies. They stayed in positions that no one living could endure. A couple were embracing fraternally. Others grinned at one another with stretched features. The Runner hurriedly let go of the plank again.

He squatted in the sand till the cloud of dust had gone on round the corner. Then the clatter of approaching shells got him going again. Once more, signs flew towards him, guns, stacks of empty cartridges. Passed him on the edge of the road. Remained behind.

At last began the field with the thistles and the patches of wet that never dried out. And then the endless rows of birch crosses. The mortuary cart stopped at the edge of the cemetery. A bunch of shavenheaded figures were busy with shovels. A few were tugging at the back of the cart. Others lugged a corpse through the grass.

After the last row of graves the village began. Either side of
the track, low huts, block houses of unfinished logs, roofed
over with weathered shingles. A well with a pump handle.
Beside it, on a pole, the tin banner of the battalion.

The Runner staggered into the building. The Adjutant
stood in front of a door. He pressed his hand against his steel
helmet, and pulled the reports from his leather satchel.

From that instant, the Runner began to sleep. He turned
round automatically, reeled back along the corridor, put his
feet like a sleepwalker on the steps going down. Half in a
dream, he collapsed on to the rough wooden bench next to
the well. Exhaustion covered him like a black pall. From the
company command-post to battalion headquarters – mission
accomplished.

1

The Adjutant balanced the company reports in his hand. He read the names of men who were no longer extant, deleted concepts, constituents of the past. Lost: item, 1 machine gun, serial number no longer possible to ascertain; item, 2 belts; item, 1 replacement barrel; item, 1 NCO; item, 7 men. There was little sense in submitting these reports to the CO. He and the CO were the hinges of life. The door opened: names arrived. The door closed: names departed. Here, life was given a number, and death a number. It was up to them to learn to cope with it. He had his job. What the CO had, he didn't much care to know.

He knocked on the door. It was lined with cardboard, no one knew why. Maybe in a bid for respectability. Or maybe the door was split, or the cardboard was to show that this was the door to the CO's office.

The Major sat at a desk covered with papers. You could see he was exhausted. He sniffed the mouldy smell of the building, a mixture of cold smoke, rotten wood, dirty laundry, sweat and vermin. It was a while since he'd last shaved. Two days, even a week. He was like a dead man whose beard continued to sprout. Anyone could see how long he'd been lying out. He had a glass eye, which disfigured him. His real eye looked along the four table legs in turn; at the cans full of water, at the yellowish liquid that had dead cockroaches swimming in it. He was trying to work out whether the cockroaches were getting more numerous. It was a mechanical census, he didn't really care either way. It was a long time since he'd last attended to the stiff forms floating in the liquid.

When the Adjutant entered the room, the Major busied himself with appearances. He registered a spider's web on the smooth paper covering of the table. A wheel, clock weights. Clocks ticking, fast or slow, but incessantly endeavouring to shorten a life's span.

While he observed them tensely, as if they would reveal a secret to him, he felt like something bobbing in the water, lifeless. He felt wet on his skin. He started to swim. He felt better. When he woke out of this condition, the pain returned. It was an unendurable pain that he couldn't do anything about. It felt to him as though he'd been living in it for ages already. It hung on his movements like lead. Incessantly the words in the telegram banged in his brain: 'ANNA AND CHILD DEAD STOP BURIED UNDER DEBRIS OF HOUSE STOP BODIES UNRECOGNIZABLE STOP IMMEDIATE BURIAL.'

He didn't know where the telegram was, he had mislaid it somewhere. But he couldn't shake off the pain. When the Major sat at his desk alone, he would think about it. ANNA AND CHILD DEAD. He stared at the dirty walls. He opened his mouth and couldn't speak. Sweat came out on his brow. All he could remember of Anna was that she had black hair. He couldn't put a face to her any more. And they had lived together for twenty years. For twenty years they had seen one another every day.

He went to bed with her at night, and in the morning kissed her on the mouth. But he could remember nothing of her beyond the one thing: she had black hair. With the child, he at least had a photograph. A summer day in the garden. Flowers in the sun. Alert vivacious eyes laughing back at him. Caught in the camera lens. His dead daughter.

The Major suppressed a giggle, and looked out through a cracked piece of window glass. The Runner was lying stretched out on the bench. The sun was going down. Clouds of midges hung in the air. Everything was the way he had expected it to be. The street, the well, the sun's fiery disc on the horizon. A soldier walked past in strikingly white fatigues, and spat expressively in the sand. Everyone he knew was still alive. Only his daughter was dead. As though he had failed to pay a bill. Now – unexpectedly, ruthlessly – she had been cashed. That was the thanks he got, that was justice.

He turned and issued a command: 'I want the Runner in here!'

'Yes, Major!' replied the Adjutant's voice. A draught picked three pieces of typing paper off the table, and deposited them on the floor.

As the Major bent down to pick them up, he looked out through the dirty window again. He saw how the Runner, addressed by the Adjutant, picked himself up, slipped by under the window frame, and suddenly materialized in front of him in the room.

'At ease,' said the Major, purely from habit. The Runner,

worn down by daily orders, was standing pretty slackly in front of him, as it was.

'All well?' asked the Major. As he did so, he thought of his dead daughter. A tragedy with unpredictable consequences. Each time, something else came along that he'd failed to think of.

The Runner said: 'Yes, sir!'

'And the log-road?'

The Adjutant hurriedly intervened: 'That's no longer defensible!' He moved alongside the Runner. For a moment, they looked at one another. Two men making some sort of deal with one another. Silently, no words.

The Major fell into a rage: 'Interesting.'

'Yes.' The Adjutant inspected his fingernails. 'Exposed point. No one's fault.' All at once, he looked up. 'I'll draft the memo to divisional HQ right away!'

Outside on the street, a heavy traction engine rattled by. The floor shook. A sprinkling of dust came down from the ceiling. A piece of glass fell out of the window pane and shattered on the wooden floor.

'Presumably they're reinforcing the artillery regiment,' observed the Adjutant.

'Which one?' The Runner's question came out like a shot from a gun.

The Major irritably ordered: 'You don't talk except when I ask you a question!' He turned to the Adjutant. 'Can you get me the map please.'

The Adjutant fiddled around on the table. Under his field tunic he wore a shirt with cuff links. They were both grimy. A grey line was visible along the creases.

With a show of indifference, the Runner looked at the map.

The Adjutant's voice was saying: 'After all, we owe it to our men.' His hand gestured vaguely at the table. It wasn't clear what he meant.

'Owe?' repeated the Major. He looked at the Runner, and shook his head.

'I am convinced, sir,' said the Adjutant in a businesslike tone of voice, 'that our point of view will be accepted.'

'What do I care!'

'I beg your pardon?' The Adjutant spluttered in embarrassment.

The Major repeated stubbornly: 'I said: what do I care!' He clasped his hands together, and felt a clammy moisture, as of someone running a temperature. He might look up the doctor. For a moment, he toyed with the notion. He'd have little trouble convincing the fellow he was ill. With a sense of aggrieved innocence he thought: and I really am too.

'You want to smoke?' the Adjutant turned to the Runner. 'That's fine by us!' He felt like a diplomat, at ease everywhere – regardless of the circumstances.

'Thank you!'

The Runner awkwardly filled his pipe. When he was done, he didn't light it. He didn't want to take any chances. A blue-bottle that had been crawling about on the stove suddenly took flight for the window. It smashed against the pane, and fell to the ground. There was a scampering as rats under the roof.

'What were we talking about again?'

'Counter-attack or not?' the Adjutant replied unexpectedly. He dangled his question at the Major like a painting at an auction. Going. Going. The Adjutant had already given instructions: no counter-attack, no sacrifice.

The Runner looked hard out of the window, and listened
to every word.

'But you know the orders,' said the Major.

'What orders, sir?'

'To hold our position. Any enemy breakthrough is to be
mopped up in a counter-offensive!'

'Yes of course, of course,' responded the Adjutant, half-
apologetically. There were hundreds of orders. Orders are
orders, and they have to be obeyed, but sometimes one might
just slip your mind.

The Major thought about his daughter. It was only fair if
others got telegrams as well. He thought: I must get my own
back. His hands still felt as wet as if he'd dipped them in
water. Revenge can ease pain. He wanted to take revenge.
'No exceptions,' he said, and caught the Runner staring at his
glass eye, as though expecting it to fall out.

'Major!' The Adjutant pointed at the map spread out on
the desk. With his finger he traced a black line that led
through the swamps. 'The log-road is worthless. It's not a
road. It's a track made out of tree branches.' He pointed at a
red cross. 'That machine gun is in a needlessly exposed position.'

The Major didn't want to hear any more. He knew what
was coming. The futility of the position. The narrow path
through no man's land. Thin boughs, laid side by side. No
direct communication with the rest of the company. Bog
squirming up between the branches. The Russian machine
gun was trained on the path. A screen of foliage provided
visual cover, but not protection. A continual hail of explosive
rounds passed over this one and only link. As for the position
itself: a tangle of uprooted trees, stumps and stripped bushes.

No craters. The swamp filled any shellhole within moments. A miracle that the unit had lasted as long as it had.

'And the company's strength is way down. We need every man. How can you justify a counter-attack?' the Adjutant concluded. He took his hand off the map. He waited for a reply. Only now did the Runner grasp what they were talking about.

It was hard for the Major not to let on. He kept having to think of his daughter. His daughter had been killed. He mustn't forget that. He could have said it to the Adjutant's face. Why me? What have I done to deserve that? I never had a house built for myself in French style, like the artillery colonel. You can see it from the window. It's down there. His gunners are living in holes in the ground. I don't have officers' parties every day with candelabra and white porcelain. I don't keep a mistress. I don't allow official trips into the back country. I've got nothing beyond my concern for my battalion. I never wanted this campaign. I'm a private citizen. They killed my child. I'm finished with being your guardian angel . . .

'Can you justify it?' The Adjutant repeated his question.

'We've got replacements.' The Major yelled: 'Enough replacements to bring the company up to strength.'

'Yes, sir.'

The Runner crumpled and turned pale. He recalled his hope that they would be allowed to dwindle away. Crumble. One after the other, taken back, wounded or dead. Till whoever remained would have to be withdrawn.

'Replacements in platoon strength,' said the Major, at normal volume.

The Adjutant smiled pityingly. 'Replacements,' he gestured

dismissively. 'Men without experience. You were going to keep them here, and get them toughened up gradually.'

He's going to carry on talking to me, thought the Major, till I'm sitting at the table by myself again, and see the clocks with their weights, and hear the ticking. It would calm me down, knowing that others have had losses as well. I need to hear that, otherwise I'll lose my mind. He clung to his resolve. 'You do as I say.'

'So, a counter-attack along the log-road?' On the street outside, the traction engine was making its way back. It ground past. The walls quaked. Then silence.

'I wanted . . .' The Major looked at his boots with his one good eye.

'Yes sir?' asked the Adjutant. 'What did you want?'

'Nothing.' To gain time, the Major turned to the Runner. 'What are the enemy numbers like?' A ridiculous question. The Adjutant didn't say anything. The Runner merely:

'No one knows.'

'Hm.' The Major was surprised at his own lack of responsibility. So far, he had always faced facts. His pain had made everything misty: his sympathy, his concern, the table with the tin cans with the dead cockroaches swimming in them; the clay stove that the kolkhoz farmer had left a bundle of rags on top of; the door with the leather hinges, through which the Adjutant had come with the telegram; tragedy and devastation. He thought: Why is it I can't remember *her*? There was something amiss. You don't just forget someone you've lived with for twenty years. The telegram, a blow. Either you fall to your knees and pray, and try to atone. Or else you strike back. He thought: I'll strike back. He wanted everyone to suffer for the child: the Runner, the company in the barrier position, the whole world. And yet he felt some kind of inhibition. As though he wanted to leave himself some way out. There's always a residue of cowardice. 'Copy out the divisional orders,' he commanded.

Now he knew the way to do it. It was pretty straightforward. The Adjutant did as he was told, and he seemed to understand it too. In block capitals, he copied it out, word for word. The Runner watched him.

The Adjutant held the paper up to the Major.

'Enemy breakthroughs are to be mopped up by a counter-offensive.'

'Quite so,' said the Major. He passed the piece of paper to the Runner. 'Take thirty replacements to the Front, and this memorandum.'

'Sir!' The Runner suddenly asked: 'Is that a communication or an order?' He held the paper up against the light. The Major turned on his heel. He looked at the Adjutant: 'Have the men fall in!'

The door creaked. The Adjutant's boots crunched over the boards.

'Should I wait outside?' asked the Runner.

The Major didn't reply. He stepped up to the window and studied the papered-over cracks in the glass. Cracks that went in straight lines, then suddenly, almost whimsically, skipped to the side. The future was incalculable. Chance changed its direction.

The Major looked at the village. The well stood out against the sky like a gallows. The sun was going down between the trees in the forest. It was evening. He was pleased he had paid life back. Now everything would get easier. He had to take these sort of life and death decisions.

'Might I ask a personal question, sir?' a voice piped up. The Major had forgotten that the Runner was still standing there.

'Go on,' said the Major. He still had his back turned to the Runner, and continued to study the cracked glass.

'I wonder . . .' The Runner stalled, began again. 'I wonder – I'm only just asking . . .' he said again. Then: 'Could you get me relieved?'

The Major didn't stir. It was the first time anyone had tried asking him that.

'Ever since we've been in this position,' the Runner hurriedly went on, 'I don't know how many days it is, I must have gone back and forth a hundred times. I'm not a coward. But I can't take much more of it. I can't.' He was speaking very rapidly. The melody of the path was heard in his voice. 'I don't know when it'll be my turn. The heights – it's like target practice. I'm the target. They're all aiming at me. And the forest, with the dead and the wounded. I'm tired. Sometimes I have the feeling my lungs will tear.'

The Major drummed on the window glass with his fingertips. 'Do you think the company in the trenches are any better off?'

'Yes, yes I do,' the Runner said loudly, as though afraid he might be ignored. 'I can dig in there. I don't need to go through the mortar fire. From here – back to the trench – that's the worst. Please, would you relieve me, sir.'

The Major thought: I know what he means. You can't get used to it. It's like jumping from a great height into shallow water. You can stand the swimming. But what about the leap?

'I've heard that sort of thing before,' he said. He sounded cold. He didn't want to let himself be caught off guard.

Neither by himself, nor by the man on the other side of the desk.

But the Runner persisted. 'It's unfair.'

The Major watched the replacements emerging from the village huts. One of them was already by the well. A flushed, red face, with protruding teeth. A bearing that didn't inspire much confidence. Just a silly swagger. Certainly one of those the Runner would lead to perdition.

The voice behind the Major said: 'What would be fair is if there was a new man every day.' The Major thought: fair? Killing children isn't fair either. 'Or at least once a week,' said the Runner.

The Major realized he wasn't very interested. He ducked out of the conversation: 'I can't concern myself with every individual.'

'The Captain says it was your orders that I was to keep doing it.'

'My orders? He can choose someone else any time he likes.'

'Yes sir. But he says orders are orders.'

The Runner was starting to irritate him; the way he was talking, it was as though there was only him in the world. 'I'll have a word with the Captain,' said the Major. He still didn't move. A group of men had clustered round the well. The Adjutant was numbering them off. The replacements were busy with their packs. They were carrying too much. They would only need a fraction of what they had, and not for long. At his back, the Runner made a movement. Perhaps he had moved closer to the window? The Major didn't care. He continued drumming on the window with his fingertips. Twice hard, twice lightly. Always in the same rhythm.

The Runner cleared his throat.

'Was there something else?' asked the Major. He wished he had sent the Runner out with the Adjutant.

'I can't go back in the position.'

The drumming stopped.

'I can't,' said the Runner. 'I'm sick.'

'Sick?' The Major turned round. The lie was evident on the Runner's expression.

'I can't move my legs any more. The joints are inflamed. Someone else will have to take the paper and the replacements to the Front.' He had laid the piece of paper with the copy of the divisional orders on it down on the table, and was clenching his fists. As though he had something hidden in his hands. His face and the clay stove seemed to be made of the same substance. He was silent while the Major looked at him.

'Get out!'

The Runner didn't move. Scraps of speech drifted over from the well: the Adjutant.

'Take the report!'

The Runner put out his hand and reached for the piece of paper. Not proper obedience, just a movement. The Major looked at the grey face. There were tears on it. The Runner turned about. Silently he left the room.

The voice behind the desk was gone. The Major reeled slightly as he walked back to the window. Let the Runner whinge. The replacements formed up outside in a marching column. The Adjutant raised his hand. The Runner walked up, mopping his eyes. One or two were laughing nervously. The Runner shook his head. Through the grimy window, it all looked like a film. The sound had failed. It was silent. The Runner had been crying. With rage? Or was it something else? Now the sound came back on.

'Break step – march!' commanded the Adjutant. It echoed as though from a gorge. The Runner walked out on to the village street, and the column jerked along after him. The men, the well – everything dissolved before his eyes. Why couldn't he cry? Tears were comforting. The Major saw the window glass, nothing more. The glass reflected a stranger's grimacing face. His own face.

2

The Runner left the village with the replacements. Their new leather harness creaked. A horse whinnied near the last huts of the village. The cemetery lay there abandoned. The cart with the bodies was gone. No trace of the alarming passengers.

The column behind the Runner were quiet. The Front up ahead, enclosed in gloomy forests, was similarly quiet. Night pushed itself along the horizon. Always at twilight there was silence from the Front, as it got used to the darkness. The Runner knew that. With his left hand, he batted aside a fly that had followed him from the edge of the village. His right hand was still making a fist. It clutched the paper he had taken unnoticed from the Major's desk.

The Adjutant's message to the company was in his pocket. He would throw it away later.

There was a field-kitchen installed on the edge of the forest. The co-driver was feeding fresh wood into the furnace. A few embers spilled out. The lid of the cauldron was open. The steam smelled of nothing in particular.

The forest came out confidently to meet the path. But its trunks melted away. Only a few twigs plucked at the Runner, brushed against his shoulder. He unclenched his fist to smooth out the piece of paper. He looked over his shoulder, just in case.

One of the men had broken away, and was trying to get to the head of the column.

The Runner balled up the paper in his hand again. It needed to be darker. The tree with the hanged man was coming soon. He switched to the other side of the track. The row of men made no move to follow him. They stayed on their side, and they would be in for a fright. He smiled unpleasantly.

The hanged man dangled on a long rope, as though he'd been pulled out of the water. It was already too dark to make out his features. They had switched him round only a week ago. His predecessor had been a Commissar, this one was just a simple soldier. When parties of them were found in the forest, they were shot, stragglers were hanged. They seemed to know that. Usually they kept one last bullet for themselves. That accelerated the procedure.

The first in line leaped aside in terror. He almost ran smack into the corpse. The Runner tittered. The rest of them were alerted, and made a shy detour round the body. Their first corpse, oh me oh my.

It was getting darker and darker. The sky turned bruise-black. A telegraph was ticking away in the bushes, but the Runner couldn't see anything. Sounds wafted over from the artillery emplacements in the forest. He pulled the report out of his pocket, tore off a corner of it, and let it flutter to the ground.

The remains of the cart with the mouldered leather harness

loomed across the path like a ghost. No one noticed the paper flutter to the ground. It wouldn't be long before he'd got rid of the rest of it. Pieces of the report kept fluttering off into the dark, into oblivion. That was part of his plan. Before long, he had just one tiny bit left. He rolled it up between his fingers, and flicked it away, anywhere. A spent rifle bullet whined feebly through the treetops and knocked against a trunk. The Front seemed to be coming to life.

The soldier behind him caught him up at last. He was panting, as if he was carrying a box of ammunition as well as his rifle and groundsheet.

'I'm a baker,' he said.

A spray of tracer fire clattered into the boughs. The Runner pulled on his steel helmet, which thus far he'd carried on his belt. The voice at his side said nothing. Then after a while, it began again:

''m' baker!'

'Yeah,' said the Runner. He wondered if it was his name or his profession.

'I wanted to get in with the field bakery,' the voice explained.

'That'd be nice,' replied the Runner. He thought about bread. Fresh bread, still warm from the oven. He wasn't hungry. He thought about starched aprons, a tiled kitchen, a floury warmth.

'Back home, I've got my own bakery with my own mill,' the voice went on. And then, sounding very sorry for itself: 'I was cheated.'

'We've all been cheated,' said the Runner. His voice was drowned out by the whistle and hiss of a shell that detonated in the forest.

'Keep going!' shouted the Runner, but the men had all flung themselves to the ground. The baker was stretched out as well.

'Get up!' the Runner yelled furiously. He thought: What have I let myself in for; this shower would rather creep along on all fours. A minute passed, and finally they were all up. They went on.

'A bakery with a mill,' the voice next to him resumed. A parachute flare opened out over the forest. Its bright illumination pierced through the ragged treetops. For half a minute they were running through white light.

The Runner turned to look the voice in the face: a row of protruding teeth, and an expression of stupidity. Then night drew its curtain once more.

'I'll see you come out of it with something too,' wheedled the voice. 'A word from you . . . I'm sure you know who to talk to. The place for me's in the field bakery. Everyone should serve where he's most useful.' The last sentence swollen with false conviction. 'I don't know anyone.' The Runner gestured irritably. He realized he still had in his hand the piece of paper from the Major's table. 'Fall back. We need to keep distance, it's about to get dangerous.' He wanted to be alone. The shadow obediently fell back. He was able to think, and to smooth out the paper. The Major wouldn't miss it. He only collected bits of paper like that in order to destroy them. He knew what was written on it by heart. A vehicle blocked the path. Wounded men were being picked up. He tripped over a stretcher. Someone swore. He dropped the paper. It took him a while till he found it.

The file behind him was getting out of order. One man walked into him. Others shouted: 'Runner, Runner!' He lined them up again, and found himself getting out of breath. For safety's sake, he shoved the piece of paper in his pocket. In the event of a checkpoint, he could claim he was carrying it in case of emergency. Of course that was also forbidden, but they didn't mind quite so much. Thousands of such bits of paper came out of nowhere. He had never seen it happen, but he was sure they were dropped from aeroplanes. Sometimes they were seen caught in the treetops, or on the shingle roofs of the village huts. Most of them were scattered over the swamps, where they were no good to anyone. There were blue ones and pink ones. Both carried the same message.

COME OVER TO OUR SIDE, COMRADE! THIS PASS GUARANTEES YOU LIFE AND LIBERTY! On the back side of it was something in Cyrillic. He couldn't make it out. One man in the company had translated it. It didn't sound bad. 'Anyone who produces this form is a deserter. He is entitled to privileged treatment, life, liberty, and passage home at the war's end.' No one in the company took it seriously. The Runner didn't really either. And in spite of that, most of them had one of these 'passes'. This one here came from the Major's table. The assault on the log-road would take place without the Runner.

The business with the report was taken care of. No one would ever find the scraps of paper. There was another flare up in the sky. Through the foliage overhead, the Runner watched it slowly subside. He wondered how far there was to go. But there already was the shadow of the railway embankment. A machine gun started rattling away. It was as if the embankment had only been waiting for him. As on command, the sentry nearest him fired back. The next man joined in. Fire ran down along the tracks like a burning fuse. Hissed and crashed. The rail seemed to be shaking with fever. From down in the dip, a second machine gun suddenly opened up. Everything was popping and banging, it was like a New Year celebration. Further off was the firework of the flares. And suddenly, the noise collapsed in on itself like a house of cards. Silence. Just one ricochet whistling though the air. It seemed to have taken off vertically, and wouldn't be back.

'Time for a cigarette,' the Runner said to the men. They stood around him. The little luminous red dots glowed. Each time someone drew, vague features became visible. From the heights opposite, a few shots clacked over at them.

'All right then,' said the Runner, and tossed his cigarette end under the trees. The file whisked off along the embankment, with the Runner in the lead.

There was some traffic on the path. Men carrying crates of ammunition squeezed past them. Another Runner overtook them. At the dressing-station, there were some black clumps on the ground. Dead men. His column didn't make a squeak. Behind a canvas drape was the whitish gleam of a carbide lamp. It smelled of carbolic and quicklime. Far off in the forest, a battery was firing. In the reddish sheen of the detonations as they flickered over the night sky, the Runner for a second glimpsed the outline of the height, the pylon, the scorched earth of the slope, the cratered field. The enemy was sending out breathless bursts of machine-gun fire. High-explosive shells drenched the rails like a thunderstorm. Finally, they broke off, with a vicious satisfaction, as if to say: There's more where that came from.

The slope began. The Runner clambered on to the

·embankment, ducked his head, and started to run up the hill. The trench-mortar detonations were like falling rocks. At once he was in the thick of it, the file of replacements following him likewise. But he was only thinking about himself. An inner voice called out: 'Drop!' He lay on the deck. It decreed: 'Run for all you're worth!' He ran. His legs obeyed his instincts. The height was like an erupting volcano. Stones, earth and sand clattered over him, a lava rain of incandescent splinters. Sudden quiet. Nothing. Just a fluorescent screen, hanging in the air.

He stood upright, and didn't dare throw himself down. His life depended on a single movement. The sense that there were a hundred rifle muzzles aimed at him in the darkness made him tremble. His teeth chattered. The fluorescent screen grew brighter all the time.

'Drop,' whispered the voice of temptation. He couldn't even breathe. The only part of him to move were his eyes. They tried to penetrate the darkness, to see the rifle muzzles that were pointing at his chest. The beam of the fluorescence flickered, it was like a headlamp. Other than the pylon, he was the only upright thing on the hill. The replacements were hunkered down in the shadow somewhere. The beam wouldn't go out.

'You'd better drop now,' determined the voice of temptation. The flare went out, and he sprang forward with relief. Like a blind man, he went smash into the concrete. His hand groped in shards of glass, and his knee was full of burning pain. Something looming and dark – one of the pylon supports – threatened to fall on top of him. But it didn't fall, and he stopped for breath in the lee of the concrete shelter.

With the line of men who were trailing along after him, he couldn't pay a visit to the hole under the foundations of the mast. He was a convict. Got out of jail. Wherever he might stop and look for shelter, he was followed by a gang of other convicts, who were using his escape route. The only thing open to him was to plunge forward into the darkness again.

It was easier, going downhill. Gravity helped him. He was like a ball, bounding down the slope in great leaps. A clattering as of wooden clogs on an iron bridge accompanied him: rifle-grenades feeling for him. A branch whipped across his face. He was already in the brush down in the hollow. His feet no longer obeyed him. In the shrubbery he defecated, like a man able to think of his body again, once he has done his duty. He always defecated in the same place, and there was never a time he couldn't do it. In that respect, he was like a dog. A drumming of sixty feet came down after him. A locomotive of human bodies, driven by fear and panic. He had trouble getting them to stop. It surprised him there was no one missing. They crossed the overgrown hollow together. Twigs and thorns pierced the uniforms, and dug into the skin. They reached the beginning of the trench. Bullets buzzed like bees through the foliage.

The Runner said: 'Wait here till I come for you!' He normally ran the last stretch to the shelter, even though there was no evidence of mortar fire here. With relief, he pulled aside the metal cover at the entrance, pushed his way through the crack, and took a breath, before lifting aside the ancient piece of sacking.

The smell that greeted him was like poison gas. Even before he could see the enemy, he smelled him. The disinfectant clung to their uniforms, whether they were living or dead.

'A deserter,' announced the Sergeant, with an expression on his face as though he had personally pulled him out of the enemy lines.

The Russian soldier sat on the bench facing the table, and the Captain was pressing against the other side of the table. They fixed one another, as though each waiting for the other to pull out a knife. The Russian had slitty eyes, bitten fingernails, and he was scared. His cropped hair stuck straight out from his scalp.

Finally the Captain broke the silence: 'We're not getting anywhere like this. This man is disturbed!' He scratched his head, and decided: 'I'm going to draw a diagram!' He paid no attention to the Runner. With the aid of a piece of paper and a pencil that he usually chewed on, he wanted to learn where the Russian mortars were situated. No success. The man gazed silently at the piece of paper, and shrugged his shoulders. The smell of his uniform infested the shelter, which stank as it was, of sweat and shit. The Sergeant raised his hand. 'Maybe he'll understand this better?' he asked, and slapped the round stubbly skull.

'No,' said the Captain, 'don't hit him!' He looked at him. The Russian soldier smiled, without understanding.

The Sergeant rapped against his holster: 'Here's something he might understand better.'

The Captain appeared to give up: 'He doesn't know anything. Can't be helped.'

Smiling, the other fished a few shreds of tobacco out of his trouser pocket, tore off a corner of the diagram, and rolled himself a cigarette. He pinched the end together, to keep the tobacco from spilling out, leaned forward over the candle, and began to smoke.

'Does that shit taste good?' asked the Sergeant sarcastically.

The soldier beamed: a broad, childlike or peasant beam. He looked at the faces of his enemies, and thought they were not unlike his own, different faces, but just as fearful and suspicious. Their desires were as reduced as his: a bit of food, warmth, an end to suffering. Suddenly a change came over his face. He looked perplexed, as though he had to say thank you for the consolation he hadn't received, the blow on the skull, the gesture with the pistol. He spread out his arms. They seemed to want to take in everything. The barrier position, the plateau, the sector of the Front, the whole land, presently covered in darkness.

The candle flame shrank. The Captain jumped. The Russian sat silently on his plank bench and smiled. But a change had taken place.

'They're planning to attack,' the Sergeant blurted out. In his mind's eye, he could already see figures rising up out of the trenches, a play of shadows and abeyances, a swarming human wall following a hail of explosives.

'My kingdom for an interpreter,' said the Captain, reaching back to his days as a schoolmaster, as though he might find some security there.

'He'd better go to battalion headquarters,' said the Sergeant.

Fine, thought the Runner, back to headquarters. He forgot he'd meant never to go that way again, that he hated the plateau. Now he would manage to get away from the offensive. A present from fate. He smiled contentedly. The enemy soldier smiled too. There was nothing in the world that didn't make sense. As he had always thought. God and a just world. The Sergeant's voice dribbled in his ear. He didn't listen. He already saw himself running across the plateau with the prisoner, avoiding the danger. The woods would give them shelter. The Sergeant's face loomed towards him. A hand patted him on the shoulder.

'I'll take him back, you're tired.'

The Sergeant's voice was soothing and soft.

The Runner saw the Captain sitting in his place, swimmily saw the smile of the enemy soldier.

'No,' he protested.

'Yes, yes,' said the Sergeant.

Suddenly the Runner had a vision. He saw the Sergeant leaving the shelter with the enemy soldier. They trotted out into the pitch-black night. The Sergeant had drawn his pistol, the prisoner responded to the merest pressure on his back. A sentry in the trench challenged them. 'I'm taking him back to battalion headquarters,' the Sergeant replied. Their shadows advanced along the saps, and brushed the bushes in the hollow. They stumbled up to the plateau. The Sergeant made the prisoner walk along in front of him. A long, long way. They walked through mud, craters, over sand. They got smaller . . .

'I brought some replacements from the battalion,' the Runner heard himself say. But the Sergeant had already left the shelter with the prisoner.

It was dark as it always was, in the hole under the concrete underpinning. The Corporal was crouching between his two comrades. They lay wrapped in mouldy blankets on the wet earth. Their breathing rattled. The cold night wind blew through the entry. The Corporal was on watch, and, because he was tired, he lit his pipe. Everything on the plateau was quiet. There was no dull shell crump. The hammering of rifle fire was silent. The Corporal cocked his ear, but no mortars came thundering through the night. Time crept on. He waited. The unfamiliar silence irked him. It was as though there was electricity in the air.

The Corporal stood up, and stumbling over his two comrades made his way to the exit. Slowly he pushed himself through the hole. A light breeze riffled his hair. The pylon overhead was humming. A bit of steel that shells had ripped out of its mooring left a black shadow in front of him. The wind carried a sound from the enemy positions. As though a lorry was trying and failing to get up a hill. Far left, silent sprays of tracer drifted through the night. A rain of sparks that fell into the water and went out. Only afterwards could he hear the thump of their firing.

The Corporal reached for his flare pistol. There was fresh dew on its leather holster. The lock clicked. He stretched out his arm, and pulled the trigger. A dull thud. The flare hissed away, and a second later, it was a shooting star over the barrier position. A comet flying towards the enemy trench. There, its parachute opened. In the harsh magnesium illumination, the Corporal saw he hadn't aimed high enough. Instead of illuminating the plateau, the fluorescent screen hung over the hollow. Ahead of him were the dead positions. Nothing stirred, not a breath of life. A graveyard in moonlight. Tree stumps like gravestones. A pool of water like an ornamental lake without water lilies. The labyrinthine windings of the trenches. The vegetation like a cemetery wall. The fluorescence sank further. On the ground, the light gradually sputtered out. The Corporal rested his submachine gun on the parapet, and waited. He took off the safety catch. The pylon was humming. His wristwatch ticked. Suddenly out of the darkness came the sound of shuffling feet. He straight-away pressed the gunstock to his shoulder. As a flash of fire passed over the hill from the artillery positions, he saw a figure. A soldier in enemy uniform was advancing towards him.

Even before the light faded, the Corporal had pulled on the submachine-gun trigger.

'Don't shoot, comrade!' came a yell.

Immediately, the Corporal swung the muzzle up in the air. The soldier in front of him crumpled to the ground. Unendurable silence. The Corporal felt sweat beading on his brow. His hands shook. Suddenly the voice of the Sergeant asked out of the darkness:

'Is he dead?'

'Yes.'

The Sergeant climbed out of his crater hole, and walked up to the Corporal, who felt tempted to lower his sights a second time.

'Who was that?' asked the Corporal.

'Just a prisoner.'

'Handy human shield, I suppose.'

The Sergeant was now standing directly in front of the Corporal, and could make out the submachine gun. 'Don't worry about it,' he said after an awkward silence, but he took a step to the side, just in case. 'Good night,' he called out, uncertainly. Then he rounded the base of the pylon, and van-ished into the blackness.

The Corporal fetched the shovel to cover the Russian's body with soil. The pylon hummed in the wind. The tractor noise from the enemy trench was no longer audible. Back in his hole in the ground, the Corporal lay down on the earth and chewed his fingernails in anguish.

3

The stable door fell shut behind Captain Zostchenko. He stopped, and stared out into the darkness. His eyes took some time to adjust. He was still dazzled by the light, and he was trying hard not to think about Sonia, who was lying inside. He couldn't even make out the forms of the Siberian storm troop who had lined up on the tarmac. Somewhere, still masked by the night, there was some height that he would storm with them. Presumably just as the sun broke over the horizon, or at first light, and Sonia, in the stable behind him, was a memory to which he had to say goodbye, as if on command. In order to avoid thinking about her, he forced himself to think about the General's broad epaulettes instead. That was in the course of a meeting in Nevorosk. A staff officer read out the names of the units who were taking part in the attack. Red Star, Tractor Plant Ufa, Kolkhoz Dynamo, Lenin Rocket-Launcher Unit, Trench-Mortar regiments Moskva, Marx, Robot . . .

'*Are you in command of the Siberians?*'
'*Yes, comrade general.*'

'Are you familiar with the plan of attack?'

'Yes, comrade general.'

'The tanks only go as far as the German wire. Then there's swamp. If you and your men follow the tanks, the assault will stall. That might be the end. Explain that to your men, and once you've made a breach in the line, don't forget the signal for the carriers.'

'Yes, comrade general!'

Zostchenko could remember every word. As far as the German wires. Then the swamp began. That was where the plan had a little hole. Zostchenko's battalion were to be sacrificed on the cornerstone of the enemy front. They would lose their lives in a diversionary action. Sacrificed to the greater good of the plan.

In that instant, things got going. A flame jagged up into the night. It lit up the whole bowl of the sky, from horizon to horizon. The Captain stood in the middle of a ring of fire. The earth split open and spat out hot lava. There followed a thunderbolt that left him stunned, and then the artillery regiments' salvo was under way. The rushing of the shells was like the noise of a mountain torrent. Only now did he notice the gun barrels protruding past the drawn camouflage netting. The tubes subsided, reached the lowest point, were raised up by some invisible power, spat out a new shell. Metal locks clicked.

Zostchenko saw the artillerymen by the flashes of fire from their gun muzzles. They looked serene, as if in the performance of some sacred ritual. His eyes drunk on the fiery swarms of incandescent birds, his ears deafened by din, his nerves lashed, he screamed. He made out the sunken forms of his Siberians on the tarmac. For one moment he held off, then his voice took him away with it.

The rolling barrage. The Captain looked into the staring eyes of the Runner and screamed. They both opened their mouths, and then the air pressure hurled them into the shelter. The red sky, the darkness, the other man's face – everything spun at baffling speed like the numbers on a roulette wheel round an invisible centre. Their lungs had nothing to breathe. They flopped against the walls, like bundles of clothing. That was the end. Or the beginning.

The Runner went into a dream: someone brought a bottle into the shelter, and sat down on the table. He could see the label on it, but could not read what it said. The label or perhaps the bottle was upside down. Then he felt the need to empty his bladder. But when he began to do so, he felt a burning pain in his right hand. He thought: I'm bleeding to death. He was in a cathedral. A hundred voices were singing a chorale, and the singing broke against the windows. In the middle of the church hung a gold cross. That was the peace he had always sought. His hand reached out, and he woke up. A chill inched across his back. He started. His consciousness returned, with pitiless clarity. He was gripped by fear. His fingers were gummy with blood. It was trickling out of his body into the darkness, and suddenly he understood what was happening: the arcs of shells, parabola by parabola. Projectiles calculated to land bang on the trench. A wave of steel, drilling itself into the ground, even as the next one was flying through the air, and the one after was erupting from the guns. The attack of a regiment, a division, an entire army, and the focus of the attack was just in front of his own trenches.

The ground wheeled before the Runner's eyes. The barrage was approaching. First the trench, then the communication saps, the shelter, then up the height, past the mast, down the other side, into the forest, the heavy artillery . . . It was always going to be that way. And now the finale was at hand.

A wave of air-pressure pulsed through the shelter. The Runner pressed himself to the ground. He had to wait for it either to move on, or else to bury him. Two layers of tree trunks overhead, trees a foot in diameter, and on top of that at least another eighteen inches of soil. It would last, or else it wouldn't. Sweet Jesus.

Dirt from the ceiling. Direct hit. Splintering wood. The shelter shook. The tin shield at the entrance was like a leaf in a high wind. The space under the tree trunks seemed as though it might explode. But the Runner survived. Two layers of tree trunks held out. This time. The next shell would go straight through. The Runner thought: But there won't be a next one. He wasn't green any more. They wouldn't hit the sore spot again. The barrage crept on, already it was the other side of the shelter.

He struck a match, looked at his hand. The inside of his thumb was laid open, a flesh wound, nothing more. He felt ashamed of his panic. Next to him, the Captain was groaning. The match went out. 'Captain?' he asked into the darkness. The air smelled of gunpowder. Mortar shells were exploding on the timbers overhead. He tasted bitter almonds on his tongue.

'Have you got a cigarette?' asked the voice of the Captain.

'Sure!' He reached out into the darkness with his bloody hand, and stuck it in some jam. He felt nausea. Hurriedly he pulled his hand back.

'What's going on here?!' the Captain's voice suddenly called out.

'Drum fire!' His voice sounded whiny and reproachful.

Outside, in front of the shelter, a tongue of flame licked along the trench.

'I must have blacked out,' said the Captain. Splinters and stones pattered against the tin plate at the entrance. The Runner hurriedly reported: 'I'm wounded.' He pulled himself into an upright position, and groped along the wall. It was shaking incessantly, like the plate over a motor. The earth was cold and damp. The shelling had reached the little dip at the foot of the hill. He could tell from the echoey explosions. Small-calibre mortar shells were coming down all the time on the beams of the shelter.

'Can't you strike a light?!' There was irritation in the Captain's voice. He ordered: 'Call company headquarters!'

The Runner felt around for the field-telephone. He groped over the ground. The table was gone. Splinters of wood everywhere. At last he had the bakelite box in his hands. The earpiece had fallen out. He cranked the handle and listened. Not a sound from the receiver. 'There's no connection, Captain!' As he waited, he felt along the wires with his hands. An arm's length away, they closed on fresh air.

Feebly the Captain said: 'Can't you try and get some light!'

'I can't find the lamp!'

'Good God,' said the Captain, 'surely you'll be able to lay your hands on a candle!'

Time passed. Only the storm outside continued to rage with unabated ferocity. The noise swelled and ebbed away again. The Captain had managed to find a tallow light. Once the flame was lit, it barely cast a shadow. On the ceiling, the network of branches flickered a little. Earth continued to trickle down. The Captain squatted down on the ground. He asked: 'What's the matter with your hand?'

'Laid open. A shell splinter. Burns like fury.'

'I can't let you go over something like that!'

The Runner nodded. 'I know.' He tried to smile. It was all he could do, but it came out as a contorted grin. A handful of stones came rattling through the entrance. In shock, he raised his hand.

'Direct hit,' said the Captain.

Outside, it sounded as though heavy goods trains were repeatedly colliding. That was followed by a pause for breath, a short alarming silence, and out of the silence, a high-pitched scream. It came from the trench further forward, broke against the entry to the shelter, and died away. The death-cry of a man spread-eagled one last time, before the black blood vomited out of his mouth. The Runner stared into the flame of the tallow light, as though he'd heard nothing. The Captain made a self-protective motion with his hand through the air. Then the pair of them stared up at the ceiling, where the tree trunks were being slowly shredded by the mortars. Time trickled on. Each quarter-hour seemed to stretch out indefinitely. Once, by way of a change, it rained rockets. Large-calibre shells gonged in between. A slim stripe of light at the entrance to the shelter showed morning was breaking. It was pale and lifeless, the colour of a funeral shroud.

Suddenly a shadow loomed at the entrance. A form reeled in. The Runner saw the bleeding stump of an arm against the filthy uniform. It was moving, as though the missing hand was still trying to find something to hold on to. A voice moaned:

'Comrades . . .'

Then he stumbled, and the Runner caught him. The other man's blood wet his hands. He looked for a leather strap, and tied up the stump. Sweat ran down his face. The wounded man watched him as though he was working on a piece of wood. He shuddered with horror, as he tied a bandage to the lump of meat.

The wounded man giggled. He said: 'If I manage to get out of here, I'll have done it.' He added happily: 'For good!' The Runner gazed at the bandage, already reddening, and said nothing.

'I'm going to try and make a dash for it right now,' the wounded man assured them determinedly, and sent a hate-filled look outside, at a cloud of gunpowder smoke that was just passing. 'I want to go over the hill immediately!' he said, sounding very determined.

'Sit down!' The Runner indicated a pallet in the corner.

'No one's got the right to detain me!'

'I know.'

'Then I can go!'

'Yes.'

'Well, then . . .' the wounded man bit his lips, reeled, and slid to the ground. He said whitely: 'If they attack, it'll be too late for me.' Shaken with pain and despair, he was convulsed with sobs. There was blood on his tunic, blood on his face, blood everywhere, only not in his lips.

'When the attack's over, we'll take you back,' said the Captain. His voice was uncertain. The wounded man shook his head. 'You don't know!'

'Know what?'

'The company's gone!'

The Runner turned to look at the Captain. The mortars continued to knock against the tree trunks roofing the shelter. A lump of earth came off the wall, and smacked on to the floor.

'What's it looking like?' asked the Captain.

'Bad.' The wounded man tried to pull himself into an upright position, couldn't do it. The Runner pushed a tarpaulin under his head. 'The flame-thrower . . . A direct hit. The unit were roasted.' His breath came hard. 'There's just lumps of meat left around the machine gun. Matz – shrapnel in the back of his head, died on the spot.' Pain shook him. 'Hager's still alive . . . but . . . we couldn't bandage him up. His intestines are hanging out.'

The Runner flinched from an explosion close to the shelter. When he looked up at the wounded man's face again, it was crying silently.

'All I saw of Fadinger was his hand,' the wounded man shut his eyes. 'It lay there in the trench as I ran back. I could tell whose it was by the ring. The pair of us wore the same ring. First, I thought it was my hand. But – I wear mine on my left hand.' He raised his intact hand, as if by way of confirmation.

'There, that's it,' he sobbed. Suddenly he pushed his hand in the Runner's face. 'Here, take it off me, will you. I can't stand to see it any more.'

The Runner pulled the ring off. If anything, it cost him more than it had to bandage up the arm stump. He tried to put the ring in the wounded man's breast pocket.

'No!' cried the wounded man in dismay. 'I want you to throw it away!'

With a reflex fear, the Runner tossed the ring in the direction of the entrance. He meant it to fly through the narrow passage, and out past the trench. However, he aimed too high, and the ring bounced against the ceiling over the steps, and rolled back.

The Runner and the Captain looked at each other. Neither felt like getting up to try a second time. They didn't move.

'When I was hit, I just ran off,' said the wounded man. 'Was there something else I should have done?'

No answer.

'Was there something else I should have done?'

'No!' screamed the Captain. 'No!' He got a grip of himself. 'I'm sorry.'

'What about the NCO?' asked the Runner.

The wounded man tried to smile.

'He's lying behind the machine gun, cursing. You know what he's like. A shell hit the munitions crates.'

'Anything in them?'

'Was,' said the wounded man.

The Runner got to his feet. He bent down and fumbled in a corner for a box of machine-gun belts. He shut the lid on it, and gripped it by the rope handles. Almost ceremonially he moved towards the entry hole. When he saw the ring lying there, he stopped.

'Leave it be,' he heard the wounded man say.

The Runner turned. The wounded man was still lying with his back to the entry. He hadn't supposed he would have noticed anything, any more than before, when the ring bounced back.

'Maybe it's a sign,' said the wounded man. 'The ring wants to stay here, and so should I.'

The Runner turned again, and crouched. With a single bound, no longer noticing the weight of the crate, he left the entry behind him. He raced along the sap. A six-foot trench was now no deeper than a furrow in a field. It was even level to the ground at times. In other places, the cover had been shorn away. He was running along a shallow stream bed, whose banks were bubbling with a mixture of steam and shrapnel. Stones rattled down. Earth spurted up. There was no point in throwing himself down for cover. There was only one thing: to get through it as fast as possible. The detonations seemed to be following him. At any moment, he thought he would feel his back being shredded. The crate got heavier by the second. Sweat and filth splashed into his face. On, on. The front line was under a white bank of fog. He ran towards it. The NCO must be lying there in the whiteness. He plunged into the fog where the skeleton of the tank lay. The firing here seemed to abate. He wheezed round the caterpillar tracks dangling into the trench – and found himself staring into a pistol's mouth.

'Are you crazy?!' the Runner screamed at the sentry.

Who dropped his weapon in shock. As if he had seen a ghost, he gawped after the Runner, who disappeared into the boiling white fogs. He ran on with his crate. Stumbled over some soft obstacle. Fell into sticky mess, and got up, feeling nauseated. Plunged on. Reached the front line. He could tell it was by the slimy boards he slithered along.

An abandoned sentry point. Only a rifle left, leaning against the breastwork. Not until now did he realize there weren't any more trench mortars chipping around like pickaxes. Damp mists looped slothfully over the position. Grim shell cavities. White froth. Smashed trench walls. Broken shelters. Ahead of him a heavy impact slammed into the wire entanglement. At his side, empty casings loomed out of the fog. Any moment now, he should be at the machine-gun emplacement. A darkish stain emerged in front of him.

He slumped exhausted next to the NCO. All he could

make out were his eyes. Everything else, his crooked steel helmet, the strings of hair, brow, cheeks, neck, his whole body was encrusted with mud.

'So it's you,' he observed laconically when he recognized the Runner.

'Here,' called the Runner. He tugged the crate of munitions on to the breastwork.

'I was just about to break off the firing-pin.'

They lifted up the tripod, and reinserted the lock in the barrel.

'How long have they stopped shooting?'

'Just a couple of minutes.' The NCO fed in an ammunition belt.

'Who's that?' There was a dead man lying on the breastwork, next to the Runner. He wanted to pull him down into the trench.

'Leave him there,' said the NCO. 'He's not pretty to look at from the front.'

'Gut-shot?'

'Something like that. Only it was shrapnel.'

In front of them, a shell ripped through the fog.

'There!' The NCO set the gun against his shoulder. The Runner stared at the gap in the fog. He couldn't make out a thing. Beyond it, some low scraps of mist were drifting over the cratered field. There was swamp between the trench and the wire. The fog overhead had turned into a sprinkling of hot steam. Translucent as glass. The gap closed again, slowly growing shut. Up in the air were gurgling shells. Further and further behind them impacts drilled themselves madly into the mud at the foot of the hill.

*

Captain Zostchenko crossed a wet meadow. In front of him was a dip in the ground. He gave the command to wait there. Their own batteries were behind them. Their detonations sounded deeper. The fire raged on with undiminished intensity, and the woods to the west were like a city in flames. He was continually tempted to believe that the attack would come off. He clung to the hope, like a naïve child. Afterwards, so the general had said, the battalion would be put in reserve on the hill. That too he put in the scales: afterwards. A word can be a temptation, whether one believes it or not.

The German minefields were sent sky-high, their entanglements were ripped, their shelters crushed. And yet, Zostchenko didn't feel any calmer. His instincts wouldn't be allayed. He pushed his way through his Red Army men, heard them talking quietly to one another, and felt their warm breath on the night air. Someone brushed against his arm accidentally. But he remained alone. Alone with his knowledge, with his critical understanding, with his oppressive memories. He brooded to himself. He shuddered involuntarily. He could feel an unpleasant pressure against his forehead, and a slight fever. His feet stomped mechanically over the ground. The hand on his watch seemed to inch forward, infinitely slowly.

As light began to break, he breathed a little more easily. On his command, a line of three hundred Red Army men moved forward. They vanished into saps, into a labyrinth of crumbling passageways and snipers' nests full of filth and rubble. The shelters contained nothing but useless weapons and empty munitions crates. The trench company had already withdrawn. A cadaver dangled over the breastworks. A blood-soaked bandage coiled in a sandy hollow.

Zostchenko trotted back, head down, to the middle of the sector, and looked at his watch again. Twenty minutes still. In twenty minutes, three hundred Siberians would rise out of the trenches and attack. In thirty minutes, the thing would be decided. The nearer the time, the more unreal the prospect seemed to him. Dozily, he grappled with the fact that his future would be decided in the next half an hour. It was like a dream. When I awake, he thought, it will all be over. He pulled himself up over the lip of the trench, and, pressed to the ground, surveyed the field. In the gloaming, he could make out the hill: a bare, lifeless form, subjected to an iron hail, and swathed in smoke and steam. The mortars were still pecking away at it. Spurting fountains of sand. Gunpowder clouds drifted over the trenches. The skeleton of the pylon still soared up into the sky. Even with all the explosions, there still seemed to be an eerie calm over the heights.

Suddenly there was a light whining. Zostchenko turned round. The sound grew louder: engine noise, mingled with the rattle of chains: the tanks. Filthy steel turrets came floating out of the fog, crashing out of the underbrush. The commandants' heads stuck out of the turrets. The earth shook. The monsters fanned out and stopped just in front of the occupied trench. In the grey light behind them, fire still quivered out of the muzzles of the artillery.

Zostchenko crooked his elbow: nine minutes more.

Lieutenant Trupikov came dashing along the trench.

'I've given orders to the battalion, Captain!' His face was impassive.

'All right,' said Zostchenko. He was struck by how level his voice sounded. He watched as Trupikov checked his submachine gun, pulled the strap of his helmet under his chin, adjusted the hand-grenades on his belt. Movements of a puppet-like stiffness, behind a misted pain of glass. The puppet was himself, crammed into a body that moved with infinite slowness. He lay down on his back, raised his arm, so that he kept both the tanks and his watch-face in view. Four minutes.

'Get ready!'

Trupikov passed the order on. The call hurried down the line, through the engine noise. Three minutes.

He shuddered briefly. Green helmets surfaced beside him. Eyes fixed him. Two minutes.

The second hand scuttled on like a little beast: hundred seconds, eighty, sixty . . .

The tanks jerked forward as their tracks tensed. Slowly they crept over the edge of the trench, hung in the air, then flipped on to the breastwork and flattened it. A wall of steel trundled past Zostchenko. He started up and plunged forward. Behind him a pack of men. The tracks chewed up the earth. Mud flew in his face. He roared in pain and fury:

'Hurrah, rah, rah!'

It was as though a horde of beaters was charging towards them. The cries caught in the damp air, and echoed away. The NCO swung the muzzle of the machine gun. He saw nothing to aim at, only the thin strokes of the barbed-wire fence, hanging like ghostly threads in the white haze.

'I'm going crazy,' whispered the Runner. Suddenly a machine gun rattled left of them. At that same instant, a dark bulk broke through the fog in front. A black colossus bobbed up towards them like a ship. And the shouting once more, behind the protective wall of the tank.

The NCO didn't budge.

'Let's get out of here!' screamed the Runner. He dropped on to his hands to scramble away.

'You're not going anywhere.' The NCO hit him on the back. The Runner lurched. 'It can only get as far as the wire entanglements. Up till now, none of them made it through the swamp.'

'We're the last. We can't keep them out on our own.' In his agitation, the Runner ran his hands over the belts, as though caressingly.

'Are you frightened?'

'Yes.'

The NCO calmly replied: 'So am I.'

'Shoot!'

The tank pushed into the wires ahead of the swamp. Stopped with a jolt.

'Now,' whispered the NCO. He aimed carefully. Left of him, rifle fire was clattering away. The machine gun was going too. Suddenly shapes spilled round the back of the tank. They pushed past it and advanced.

'Shoot!' panted the Runner.

'Get the hand-grenades ready,' ordered the NCO.

With flying fingers, the Runner unscrewed the caps. Ahead of them, with jerky movements, the brown shapes piled into the wire. They cleared a way for themselves with the butts of their submachine guns. The cover lifted on the tank turret. A leather helmet came out. The NCO switched to single shot. Aimed at the helmet. A staggering blow. It slid back into the turret. The NCO moved the lever back to repeat. He lowered the muzzle and fired a burst into the figures in the wire. They froze and looked up. One of them threw his hands up into the sky. Others reeled drunkenly. The rest of them dropped to the floor. It had taken just a couple of seconds. The bunch of men was swept away. Occasional twitchings on the ground. The NCO aimed at them.

Mud spurted up among the wire entanglements. Behind a low elevation, an arm flipped up. A hand-grenade spun through the air. It landed in the morass in front of them. The explosion died away. Brackish water splashed over their heads.

The Runner reached into the bundle on the breastwork. He jammed a wire between his fingers, ready to pull. Before he could straighten up, the NCO struck him on the arm. The Runner slipped back down. A hand reached up out of the turret the helmet had disappeared into, reached for the cover, and shut it again. From behind the tank tracks, flashes of fire spurted in their direction. A burst of submachine-gun fire rattled into the ground just in front of them.

'Damn!' The NCO let go of his gun and ducked.

'Throw, now,' he ordered hoarsely. 'Throw!'

Mechanically, the Runner ripped at the wire and threw the grenade out of the hole.

'Go on, more!'

The Runner grabbed one stick after another without waiting for the detonations, and got through them all.

'Enough,' said the NCO. A couple of grenades were still in front of them. Cautiously, he lifted his head up. He saw the tank's gun levelling exactly in their direction.

'Take cover!!'

But the shell was already on its way. It whistled just over their heads, and a boil of air brushed past them. An explosion behind them.

'Out of here!'

The NCO yanked the belt out of the gun. He took it from its tripod, and leaped into the trench.

'Left,' he yelled.

The Runner banged the lid of the munitions crate down, and reached for the ropes. Then the hinges gave way, and the contents of the crate rattled into the trench.

'Leave it!' The NCO was already running – the machine gun cradled in his arms like a baby – along the sap. The Runner picked up the two hand-grenades and set off after him.

The NCO stopped. One of the replacements was lying in front of him. He had his eyes closed, and seemed to be sleeping. A thin line of red ran out of his mouth like a silk thread. His fingers gripped his submachine gun.

'Take it off him!' ordered the NCO.

The Runner bent down. The dead man's fingers didn't want to give up the weapon. He had to tread on his arm.

'And the ammunition.'

He rolled the dead man on his side, and pulled the ammunition clips out of the canvas pouches on his belt. Behind them, where they had just been, a flare went up.

'They're already in the trench.' The NCO was in a hurry to be gone.

'No,' said the Runner. He stood up straight, looked at the NCO. 'I'm going to surrender.'

The NCO laughed sardonically in his face: 'Idiot! You and your pass, eh?'

'I don't care.'

The NCO dropped his gun. Before the Runner understood what was happening, he felt two slaps across his face, left, right.

'By way of goodbye,' the NCO explained pleasantly. He picked up the submachine gun, turned and ran on. The Runner watched his back. Hand-grenades were going off behind him. Then he started running too. In a little while, they both stopped.

The sound of crying was coming out of a dugout in the trench wall. The NCO stooped, and pulled a soldier out by his boots. It was another of the replacements. The Runner identified him by his protruding teeth. His eyes were damp and puffy. In the night, by the light of flares, he hadn't looked that different.

'Wounded?'

The question was redundant. There was a fist-sized hole in the hip of his field-tunic. A gauze dressing, scrunched into a ball, slid out of it.

'Take me with you . . .'

Without a word, the NCO picked him up. He left the machine gun lying there, and loaded the replacement over his shoulder. They ran on. The wounded man stopped crying. Only when the NCO stumbled did he groan.

The hammering of the machine gun ahead of them got louder. The NCO started to call. It sounded monotonous, as though he was steering a boat through fog. 'Don't shoot – don't shoot!' Again and again, at short intervals.

'Who's there?' they suddenly heard behind a corner.

'Password?' the NCO asked the Runner.

'Dresden.'

'OK, you can come in.'

The man was standing behind a canvas-wrapped pile that blocked off the trench. A couple of others were leaning against a Russian machine gun mounted on the cover.

'A mighty fortress is our God,' said the NCO, while he pushed the wounded man across the pile.

'Have they got into the trench yet?'

'I think we're the last,' said the NCO, and got into the defensive position. He pointed behind him, where the machine gun was rattling away that they had heard before.

'What's happening up there?'

'They're mounting a frontal attack, under cover of fog. But they won't make it. They'll get stuck in the swamp and we'll mow them down.'

'OK,' said the NCO. 'I'll take over command here.' He watched as the Runner entered the position after him. He dislodged the canvas cover and shrank back in horror. A pile of inert forms slithered out. The corpses had been stacked up into a protective wall.

'Jesus Christ,' gasped the Runner.

'Don't worry about it,' said the NCO. 'The Almighty must approve, do you think He'd allow it otherwise?' He awkwardly lit a cigarette. The 'Almighty' sounded unpleasantly cynical.

The Runner said nothing.

'Go and tend to the wounded, but don't tell them we're surrounded, or that there's no chance of ferrying them back.'

The Runner went into the sap.

'Say: yes sir!' the NCO called after him. He got no reply. The Runner disappeared into the haze. Suddenly the NCO felt a little sorry for him.

4

In the lee of the tank, Zostchenko was firing his submachine gun at the hammering machine gun in the haze. The explosions of the hand-grenades blinded him. Then he heard a rattle against the steel treads of the caterpillar tracks. He had to throw himself on the ground.

He saw that the tank's first shell was too high, but the second winged into the heart of the machine-gun nest. The tank commander had slumped back into his turret, with a wound to the head. To Zostchenko it was all like a bad dream. Ten or twelve of his Siberians were caught in the wire with contorted limbs. In front of him fog, next to him the tank. As from a great distance, he heard the hum of the motor. He was ringed by his Red Army men, but he was alone as always. Lieutenant Trupikov hunkered in a hollow, all set to leap out. Zostchenko failed to realize they were all waiting for him, for him to set an example. He wasn't in the real world.

Soloviev had stood next to him, blinking his eyes, the way he always did. Was about to say something to him. He could see it from his eyes, his mouth. His whole face told him. But then he hadn't said it, his eyes had just grown round with shock. As if he had trodden on a piece of glass with bare feet. Not too alarmed. No expression of fear. A disagreeable surprise, nothing too terrible. And it was like that that he had received death. Zostchenko didn't know where he was hit. Soloviev sat down. Not quite like a man sitting down, but not like a man wounded either. Surprised, but content. He was already dead.

Zostchenko had watched everything, surprised and incredulous. How a man could die like that. Unprepared. Not even finish what he was thinking, or say the words his lips were forming. Where was the conclusion, the high point? Strange that the question should have come to him from Soloviev. Others had died as well. Before his very eyes. Strangers, just as strange to him as the Red Army fellows who stood around him, waiting. Waiting for what?

It was time to stand up, to make his way through the wire. Towards the layer of haze. Barbed wire. A fine drizzle . . . Just like the other time . . .

Murmansk. The harbour. The dock with iron posts and barbed wire. A soldier in the fog. His rifle barrel sparkled with raindrops. He himself, a little boy, wet through and shivering. But he was a soldier, and couldn't quit his post. Over there, in the whitish haze, the other man. Chill wind off the sea. Far off, the dull boom of a foghorn. Up and down, beside the barbed wire. A little boy in a sailor suit, playing soldiers, dreaming, soaked, going home with a temperature. Mama undressed him. Mama didn't ask. Mama held his hot little hand, and looked at him. The little boy didn't want to be left alone. He pressed Mama's hand to his lips. He clasped it hard, and Mama waited till he fell asleep . . .

★

Zostchenko climbed over the last loop of wire, his Siberians at his side. His boots sank into the marsh. He stuck to the ground, only advanced slowly. Brown puddles. Green patches of moss that hadn't received any shelling . . .

. . . *The cemetery at Murmansk. Brown puddles. His shoes sank into the mud. Mama's black coffin, covered by a moss-green drape. Four men with indifferent expressions. The bearded priest. Strangers comforting him. Mama, dear Mama. Take me with you. Don't leave me . . . Mama didn't hear him. All that was left: a heap of loose earth . . .*

Loose earth. Zostchenko saw craters, saw the shot-up machine-gun nest. He saw as through a pane of glass. He climbed into the trench, trod on a board. In front of him a crate with open lid. Munitions belts spilling out of it . . .

. . . *On the wet platform. In front of him lay his suitcase, with open lid. Clothes spilling out of it. Lots of strangers. Everyone stared at him as he stood by his suitcase. Somebody laughed. No one helped him cram the things back into his suitcase. Then the train approached deafeningly. People start to mill around. He wants to pack up his things quickly. Gets a shove. Everyone surges forward. No one takes care. A little boy in a washed-out sailor suit tries to stoop to his suitcase. Is swept away. His clothes are trampled underfoot. A mucky boot-heel drills into Mama's photograph . . .*

Zostchenko hurried along the trench. Stepped over dead German soldiers. Behind him Lieutenant Trupikov. A narrow sap opened up, in the direction of the hill. Zostchenko emptied a magazine of his submachine gun into it. In front of him a shot-up tank dangling over the trench. The sap changed direction. A form huddled on the ground. Had its hands up above its head. Zostchenko took aim. His fingers were lame. He let Trupikov take care of it. Trupikov's pistol barked out. The German soldier in front of him collapsed, hands still extended in surrender. Trupikov passed the signal pistol to Zostchenko. A purple flare went up, and a shower of stars came down . . .

. . . But when the shooting star fell through the leaves and on to the forest floor, then it wasn't a shooting star any more, but a little white tunic with gold-feathered wings. The child took the tunic, and lo, the child became an angel. It didn't feel the cold any more, and nor was it alone any more either. It floated up to join the other angels in heaven. God had called it home, just as He calls all people with pure hearts home. And that's why you should watch that your heart remain pure . . . Mama turned off the lamp, and in the darkness, kissed him on the mouth . . .

The trench divided. A wide sap led back; a narrow trench, barely wide enough for a man to squeeze through, forked right. Ahead, a machine gun was hammering away. Zostchenko took the right fork. He had to get round the back of the enemy gun. That was his duty. Trupikov led a detachment on along the sap. Zostchenko followed the windings of the trench, between damp, lofty earthen walls . . .

. . . The bare lofty walls of the orphanage. The corridor had lots of corners in it. Water oozed out of the whitewashed walls. He had to walk alone through gloomy passages. His heart fluttered. He panted for breath. Shadows clawed at him. But he had to walk on.

The male nurse had said so. Blows and punishments make men out of little children. Fear of pain, fear accomplishes much. Fear preserves order. Fear without end. The little boy walked barefooted on the cold stone flags. Above him the dormitories with three hundred children. Three hundred freezing little bodies on straw mattresses. Three hundred orphans hungry for love. The little boy had to walk, because he had been ordered to . . .

The trench had collapsed. Shells had flattened the walls. Zostchenko climbed up out of it. His uniform was sticky with sweat. He stood panting in the haze, on the shell-ploughed earth. All round him the cratered field. In front of him in the fog the chattering enemy machine gun. He is exactly behind the gunner. If it weren't so foggy, he could shoot him now. The mists part. He can see the labyrinth of the trenches. In all the places where he had run along the trench, he can now see green helmets moving. Little round pots going by, as at a shooting-stall . . .

. . . Round targets were pulled past on wires. Green targets, with a black circle in the middle. A hurdy-gurdy squeaked and scratched. Cadet Zostchenko shot at the targets with an air-rifle. Next to him stood a girl with black hair. Sparkling eyes, pouting mouth. Cadet Zostchenko didn't hit anything, because he was too excited. The girl Sonia laughed. He blushed. His uniform stuck to his skin. The girl led him away. Her hand was cool, the hand of a woman . . .

Back where Zostchenko had climbed into the trench, men were surging forward. They formed up into a row that emerged from the fog. Pairs of Red Army men were lugging tree trunks, staggering under the weight. They dropped them

into the soft marsh, and vanished again into the fog by pairs.
A silent mime. A rhythmic coming and going: a carpet for the
tanks. The carrying detail's task had been performed. The
monsters came ploughing up. The first tank slashed open the
wet ground, rolled on to the uncertain timbers. Behind it the
forms of others. They felt their way on to the trunks. Crept
cautiously forward. Already the first had reached the trench,
had solid ground under its caterpillar tracks. And the second.
The third in line started to teeter. Its tracks churned up the
trunks. Some flipped up into the air. Zostchenko heard the
splintering of wood. Chain links ground on emptiness. For
seconds. Then the tank sank. Its gun barrel tilted up. Frantic
revolutions of the tracks, grabbing for grip. The tank dug
itself a grave, sank ever deeper into the marsh. Only the
muddy turret now was above ground. The black colossus
sank. Its twin exhausts spat out a last stream of mire. The
tank immediately behind followed it into space. The third
too was unable to help itself. The gonging tone of colliding
steel plates. Three tanks drowned in the marsh. Shreds of fog
drifted past. An eerie, blotted picture. Only two of the black
monsters remained, slicing wildly across the labyrinth of
trenches, towards the hill . . .

. . . *Two people. The girl Sonia, a woman, really; and cadet
Zostchenko, who was a Captain. Not even the war was able to sep-
arate them. Was she still lying in the straw, in the stables, among
the low, steaming horses?* . . .

From out of the haze something flashed in his direction. A hot
ray laid open his hip. He jerked backwards, his fingers
cramped, agony on his face. Why could he not hear the

machine gun any more? A shadow flew at him. Tough, dirt-encrusted fingers throttled him. His shocked eyes opened on a grimace. Warm breath struck his face and knocked him back. Which was the greater – the searing pain in his hip, or his fear? He didn't know the answer.

The soldier saw that his enemy was no longer stirring. He got up. His bayonet was crimson. He wiped it on the ground, and put it back in its sheath. The tin of fuses that he had been about to open with it lay there in the trench. He looked without comprehension at the twisted form. An officer. Still breathing. Blood trickling out of the wound. A red enamel star flashed on his breast. His helmet had slipped back. Hair stuck with sweat, fingers cramping and taut. Submachine gun under his right arm. The soldier kicked it away. He knew from experience that that was necessary.

The soldier leaned against the trench wall. His knees shook. Every movement of the enemy officer hurt him. He felt the pain in the man's hip. He felt like screaming. Without taking his eye off the man's face, he reached for his carbine. Then the Russian slowly opened his eyes, and at that instant the soldier knew he wouldn't do it. The man's eyes looked astonished. They seemed incapable of understanding.

The soldier lowered his rifle, and propped it against the trench wall. He knelt down, and stroked the hand of the wounded man. The machine gun was still hammering away in the fog. The soldier thrust his arm under the Russian's head, took him under the knees, lifted him up. Reeling, he dragged himself and his burden back along the trench, in the direction of the machine gun.

5

The huts by the roadside were on fire. The wooden roof shingles or thatch glowed to white heat. The house of the artillery colonel, the house in French style, was burning on the edge of the village of Podrova. Even the pump-handle of the well was being licked at by little flames. The tin regimental colours were squeaking in the hot wind. Only the Major's hut was still cowering and intact, like a little black box, in the smoke.

The Major was on the telephone. 'I'm telling you that Podrova's in flames, even the phone line may break at any moment. The Russian artillery has been ranged on this place for the past half-hour, and low-flying planes are raking us with incendiaries. Now please understand that this isn't some local initiative, but that the Russian has gone on to the offensive.'

'Schnitzer, my dear fellow,' replied the voice on the other end of the line, 'from everything we know about the enemy here at divisional HQ, I assure you that's out of the question. It's nothing more than an – admittedly heavy – attack on the blocking position, and, as ever, that blasted hill. The general is of the view that your company will be able to regain control of the situation. He asks that you keep him abreast of developments through me.'

'I've been keeping you abreast, as you put it, for the last hour,' the Major said a little more loudly than necessary, even though the rattle of the fire was coming in through the shattered window panes, and had forced him to raise his voice a little anyway.

The man on the other end appeared to ignore the volume. 'Yes indeed,' he countered, 'but what you've had to say is nothing new. Strong enemy fire on the blocking position and the heights. The barrage moving slowly back, and for the past half-hour it's been levelled at Podrova. That's what I've been hearing from the infantry, the light and heavy artillery, the observers in your sector, the ack-ack. Now what I want to know from you is: what is your company doing? The blocking position is critical. If that collapses, we'll have to take counter-measures tomorrow morning.'

The Major ducked. A low-flying fighter swooped over the roof. Through the engine noise, he heard bursts and spurts of fire along the main street. He kept the receiver pressed to his ear. As though sitting with crossed legs at his desk, he replied: 'I seem to remember twice having informed you that we have never had direct contact with the blocking position. There is only radio contact with the adjoining infantry position on the right. And there's silence from them. It takes a runner two hours to get here from the blocking position. Even if one got through, which I would regard as an impossibility, any news he brought would be out of date.'

The speaker in divisional HQ waited while the line

crackled. He cleared his throat: 'I'm sure your situation is very difficult, but it's not up to the division to dig you out of trouble. You'll have to do that by yourself. Once you know more, give me a call.'

It sounded condescending, impatient.

The Major bit his lip. 'I'm perfectly willing to dig myself out of trouble,' he said sarcastically. 'But what I want from the ruddy division is permission for the artillery to fire. That's the only thing I ask of you!' His voice had acquired an edge of anger. 'I want my company to get the sense that something's being done for them. The other three companies have been detached from my battalion and put with other regiments. I have no more replacements. So I want the artillery to return fire. I'm telephoning because I don't have permission from the division for the artillery to fire. And I'll keep on telephoning as long as the line holds. I swear. Whether it suits you or not!'

'Schnitzer, stop playing silly buggers.' The line crackled again. 'It's three in the morning. On your account, I woke the general's orderly, and he relayed your request to the general. And I told you what he said. But that's not to say that I can wake the general every time you call. You don't know what things are like at HQ. You see things from your particular point of view. You're in the thick of things. But here . . .' the voice in the earpiece came out much louder, in a scream, but that was the fault of the line, 'here everything is as per normal! I can't break with protocol for you.'

'I see,' said the Major icily. 'In that case I just have one question!'

'Go on.'

'Am I talking to divisional HQ, or is this a lunatic asylum?'

'What's that?' The voice suddenly sounded as though it was coming through a wall.

'Never mind.' The Major hung up. The room was lit up by the brightness of the conflagration. A shadow stood in the doorway.

'What do you want?'

A light whining in the air deepened to a hum. Something whooshed and whistled over the roof. The shell burst smack in the middle of the village street.

'What do you want?' the Major repeated. A shower of earth rained down on to the roof.

The Sergeant saluted, as though he'd been summoned. He took a couple of steps forward from the doorway, into the lit-up room.

The Major stared at the man as if he were an apparition. 'Sergeant!'

'Yes, Major?'

'What's happening at the blocking position?'

The Sergeant hesitated. The Major saw his face twitch. He reached a bottle off the table, and held it out to him.

'Here, have a drink before you go any further!'

A voice on the village street moved nearer, wailing: 'Ambulancemen! Ambulancemen!'

The man passed the house. The Sergeant set the bottle to his lips. Drank in greedy gulps. Firelight flickered across his face. It was a long time before he set the bottle down. Then he looked at the Major – vacantly, as though he had nothing to say.

'Well?' The commander couldn't repress his curiosity any more.

'The Russians are attacking,' said the Sergeant, as if that explained his presence here.

The Major hesitated. He was still waiting for his report. When the Sergeant persisted in his obdurate silence, he tried to prompt him:

'What does your commanding officer have to say?'

'Well . . .' The Sergeant looked round the room, and started to sweat.

'Are you unwell?' asked the Major.

'No . . . well, maybe . . . yes.'

'Your nerves are shot,' said the Major. 'Well, that's true of every one of us.' Like a doctor, he put out his hand and took the Sergeant's wrist, felt his hot pulse. He touched the cool watchcase. 'All right now, just a few details please. Get a grip on yourself. You're bringing the very first account from the blocking position. Is the company holding out?'

'I don't know,' replied the Sergeant pathetically. There was an explosion outside. A blast of air ripped through the room. The beams creaked. When the smoke cleared, the window frames lay shattered on the floor. A confusion of maps and papers and shards of glass. The Sergeant was crouching on the ground.

'Did you catch some of that?' asked the Major.

The Sergeant got to his feet. He said: 'Report from the company, sir. Following intense artillery preparation, the enemy moved against the blocking position. The company is holding out, but reinforcements are urgently required.'

The Major looked at him piercingly. 'Come on, man, we're not on manoeuvre!' He swished his hand through the air. 'For God's sake, what is the Russian strength? Are they attacking with tanks? Have we enough ammunition, how heavy are our losses? Whatever you saw before you left, tell me.' The Major corrected himself: 'And tell me – what time actually did you leave?'

The Sergeant flinched: 'My watch stopped.'

The Major shook his head. From outside, a voice called: 'Where's the assembly point?'

The Major leaned out of the window: a roughly bandaged head. Further back in the smoke was another man propped on a stick, with an arm in a sling.

'What unit?'

The man with the head wound saw his shoulder tabs. He straightened up: 'Infantry regiment Hartmann. Light machine-gunner.'

'When did you leave your unit?'

'Why did I leave my unit?'

'When!' the Major roared at him. 'When – I want to know!'

'Over half an hour ago, Major.'

'Your unit is to the right of the hill?'

'Correct, Major!'

'Then how can you have left your unit half an hour ago?'

'That's what I did, Major. A vehicle gave us a lift.'

'What time did the Russian attack begin?'

'Must have been about eleven at night, Major, sir.'

'I'm talking about the attack, not the artillery barrage!'

A fighter roared over the roofs from the direction of the village, flying towards the front. Its machine gun was jabbering wildly. The Major identified a red star on the wing. The man with his arm in a sling rolled himself up into a ball on the street. The Major ducked under the window frame. The man with the head wound flattened himself against the wall. When it was gone, he stood up again.

'The sons of bitches,' he swore, 'they haven't started attacking yet.'

'Are you telling me that as of half an hour ago, there'd been no move?'

'Not in our sector, sir. And not left or right of us either. Nor against the hill. We would have noticed.'

'Are you quite certain of that?' the Major asked with a strange intensity.

'Yes, sir!'

'Thank you. There's a Red Cross tent at the end of the village.'

The Major slowly turned back to the room. He called: 'Sergeant?'

The room was empty.

'I don't get it,' he muttered. He walked back and forth. As if he was already out in the open. Round him bare walls. A wooden ceiling. The roof that did nothing but keep out some of the sky. Alternating hot and cold draughts through the window holes. And the rattling and crackling of the flames.

The brown telephone box which had fallen over on the desk now began to buzz.

'Command-post Schnitzer.'

The familiar voice from battalion HQ: 'Just rang back to tell you the artillery's been given permission to fire back.'

'Thanks for letting me know.' The Major's voice sounded icy.

'That's all right. We're catching it ourselves.'

'What do you mean?'

'Heavy enemy artillery bombardment of Emga. We've just had an air attack.'

'That was quick.'

'Yes, a bit of a surprise. But now we're getting our skates on.'

'That's good.'

'Not exactly,' the earpiece said in a peculiar tone. 'We're moving.'

'You what?'

'The division's relocating.'

'This is hardly the time for jokes.' The Major frowned.

'No joke,' the voice gave back. 'Just one of the facts that we deal in.'

'But with all this going on, you can't move the division!'

'Oh, the division's not moving. It's staying put. The order's going out to you that the position must be held. Only our HQ is being withdrawn slightly, or at least that's how the General put it. By the way, he was in his pyjamas as he got in the car. Thought you might like to know.'

'Unbelievable.'

'Yes,' said the voice after a pause. 'And do you know why I'm telling you that?'

'No, I can't quite make sense of it after our previous conversation.'

'You will in a minute. I have a personal command to convey to you as well.'

'What's that?'

'You are instructed to join the blocking position, to set a personal example to the fighting men.'

'Those your words?' Shells gurgled overhead.

'No. Those of a general in pyjamas. And he might have got them from a children's storybook.' The shells struck in the village. 'Bastards,' said the voice on the line. 'But you should know who you're putting your balls on the line for.'

'Pretty encouraging, isn't it?'

'Highly.' The officer in divisional HQ lowered his voice.

'Now I understand why you kept badgering me for permission for the artillery. It doesn't have to be that only the good guys die. A nod or wink at the proper moment . . .'

'True,' said the Major, 'and I won't be joining the blocking position because of the General's say-so, but because there are still a couple of decent people there, who might have some use for me. Whatever decent things we do, we do for the decent people among us. Maybe that'll help you? You could probably do with some help yourself?'

There was a click in the bakelite, but no further answer.

'Hello!' shouted the Major. He pressed the connection button twice. The line remained inert. Thoughtfully he put down the receiver, and stepped outside into the smoke-filled corridor. The Adjutant was leaning exhausted in an alcove.

'What's going on?'

The Adjutant merely shook his head, and indicated his sleeve. There was a tear in the uniform from shoulder to wrist. 'I was standing on the street when the fighter came over,' he reported shakily.

'Well, you're in luck,' responded the Major carelessly. 'I need to go to the Front. I want you to take over the battalion. Don't pull any stunts.'

'Major?'

The Adjutant looked totally bemused. But the door was already closing, and the Major disappeared into the smoke. Heat batted into his face. Somewhere in the village small-arms ammunition was going up with a rattle. He ran to the back of the building, where his jeep was parked.

'The Front!' he barked at his driver. The engine wheezed into life. The smoke draped itself round the windscreen like a protective grey cloth. Once they had left the burning village, it got better. They headed east, in the direction of the fiery horizon. The sand hissed under their tyres. They drove faster. When the cemetery came, there was suddenly a yawning crater in the road.

The driver clutched his wheel, the brakes squealed, the windscreen flew towards the Major. He closed his eyes, the jeep seemed as if it would turn over. For a split second, the world drowned in shock. Then they came to a stop between the cemetery crosses. The jeep trembled like an exhausted animal.

The driver asked stupidly: 'What now?'

'Through the cemetery!'

The crosses clattered against the bumper, and the wheels bounced among the graves. The Major felt a vague unease. Just before they rejoined the tarmac, a couple of planes flew silently out of the treetops. They banked steeply up into the air, and wheeled down in a shaking trajectory. They had spotted the grey crate in the midst of the white crosses. Little red flames spat out of the propellers. Earth spurted up. The driver was already lying pressed to the earth, in front of the radiator. The Major stared fixedly up into the sky, at the two cockpits racing towards him. Bullets tracked towards the car. Birch crosses splintered. The air grew unbearably warm, then there was a brief thrumming, and the metal of the jeep was riddled with holes. The engine noise ceased. The cemetery lay there impassively, as though nothing had happened. A pale expanse of morning sky stretched over the swaying grasses. Peace and solitude. Even the burning village somehow participated. In the distance, a charred structure collapsed without a sound. The driver lay in the grass in front of the jeep. A whitish fluid dribbled from the back of his head. The Major laid the dead man out on his back. He found it hard to close the man's eyes. He thought of his daughter. Pain, mingled with rage and help-lessness. He leaned forward, and attempted something resembling a prayer. But he could produce no sound. Only a memory surfaced in him. Something that had happened twenty-five years ago seemed to have happened only yester-day . . .

A ring at the door. The landlady announces: 'There's a lady come to speak to you.' The lady comes in. 'I've been told you were the last company commander of my son. Private Lotz. He's been reported missing.' 'Missing? That surely can't be.' The woman smiles through her tears. 'I knew it. He's alive after all. He must be in some field hospital somewhere. His letters have gone astray. The revolution. It's terrible. Do you know where he is?' Striped wallpaper. A green glass lampshade. The gloss peeling off the double windows. Shall I tell her he's dead? She has wrinkles in her face. As if someone had taken a nail to a piece of art. Etched grooves all over her face. He was her only son. 'I don't have any information for you, I'm afraid. He was wounded.' 'Well, and?' 'We got him back. The rev-olution . . . The confusion . . . You understand. I'm sure you'll hear before long.' A wounded man caught in the barbed wire. The ambulanceman is shot in the head as he tries to get him back. The company commander forbids all further attempts to rescue him until cover of darkness. By then, the wounded man is dead. 'But you were his company commander, weren't you?' 'Yes.' The mother cries. 'If you hear from your son, will you let me know.' The woman leaves, with tears in her eyes . . .

The Major got up and looked around. A black steel storm hung menacingly over the Front. The remnants of a company were fighting in the blocking position. Somewhere, women were waiting for their husbands, children for their fathers. He recalled his fatuous order, the attack on the log-road. He left the cemetery with grim determination. He selected the quickest route to the Front, the route through the swamp.

6

The Sergeant stood behind a tree, watching the figures swarming in front of the artillery Colonel's building. The roof was well ablaze, and its collapse was imminent. Soldiers were dragging boxes and cases and items of furniture out into the open. A basket of crockery came tottering out, pieces of uniform clothing were handed along a line. A couple of men tried to put out the flames, dragged buckets from the well, and emptied them over the smouldering beams.

The Sergeant recognized the soot-blackened faces. And he noticed too that the Russian shelling was moving west. The shells wailed past the ruins of the village; and exploded in the forest, among the dense trees by the sawmill.

The Sergeant stepped out from behind his cover, and cautiously looked about him. No one was watching him. He progressed hesitantly towards the village street, then, under cover of some shrubbery, bent round the back of a burned-down house. Boxes and cases lay around in the wild garden. Some exhausted men were standing together, staring into the

collapsing beams. No officer about. The Sergeant walked resolutely out. An energetic swing of the arm:

'You can't just leave that stuff lying around.'

The startled men looked at him. They saw his stripes, and
began to get to work on the chaos.

'Over here!' ordered the Sergeant, picking up a low chess-
table and taking it to the spot he had in mind. Artillerymen,
he saw they were. He felt a little out of place. When a jeep
turned off the thoroughfare, he recognized the Colonel at
once. 'Carry on!' he called. Walked with firm stride to the
jeep, raised his hand to his helmet in a salute.

'All right, all right,' the Colonel said distractedly. He
looked at the ruins of his house with irritation. 'Can you get
a car for my things?' He screwed in his monocle, and looked
at the Sergeant: 'Oh, a field engineer – well, that's very nice of
you,' he gruffed as he saw the black tabs, 'but we can manage
this by ourselves.'

The Sergeant was going to say something back, but the
Colonel had already turned away, and was giving the necessary orders. The Sergeant therefore spun on his heel and
dismissed. Where now? The village street was empty. He
drifted off to one side and rejoined it at another spot. An officer came out from between the ruins. The Sergeant squared
his shoulders. Made as though he had important business to
do. Saluted, and passed the man. He sensed the officer's
glance in his back, and he speeded up. He reached the track.
A horse and cart clattered up to him. The driver was standing
upright in front of his seat, holding the reins taut. He didn't
look at the Sergeant, and disappeared into the village in a
cloud of dust.

Brushwood beside the track. The Sergeant thought for a

little while, and decided to stay on the road. A jeep curved round the corner and raced up to him. He leaped aside. It stopped. An officer leaned out.

'Have you come from the Front? I've orders to block off any breakthrough with my battalion, but I've lost my way.' He didn't let the Sergeant get a word in. 'Podrova – am I right for Podrova?'

'Yes, sir . . .!' He pointed in the direction he'd come from. The smoking village was already obscured by the treetops. 'Another half-mile.'

'Thanks. Now where are you headed for?'

'Divisional HQ.' The Sergeant looked sternly into the officer's face. The jeep sped off. The Sergeant tramped on, but now he kept his eyes peeled on the road ahead. When a fresh dust-cloud rolled up on the horizon, he promptly jumped into the wood, and threw himself behind a bush. Marching steps, rattling gear, muffled voices. All he could see through the leaves were the boots. Infantry, evidently. Then the wheels of the support vehicles. Heavy machine guns, probably. A gap. Then more pairs of boots. An entire company. More wheels, this time light artillery. Finally, silence.

The Sergeant bided his time. Then he got back on the tarmac. Walked on, keeping to the side. From the direction of Podrova, the sounds of large-calibre explosions. Spinning shells overhead. Behind him, the soft drumming sounds of the Front. A figure appeared. The Sergeant hesitated. Marched on. A lone soldier, sweating under a heavy radio transmitter. His steel helmet bouncing along on his belt. His lank hair falling in his face. He wanted to go by. The Sergeant stopped.

'Hello there – where're you off to?'

The other set down his transmitter. With his sleeve he

wiped the sweat off his brow. 'Reserve radioman,' he replied grumpily. 'Join the artillery at Podrova. They've lost a wireless there.'

'And where are you coming from?'

'Back in the forest somewhere. They radioed us, and I had to go.' With a vague gesture, he waved somewhere behind him.

'Too bad,' said the Sergeant, and offered the man a cigarette. 'Any news of the fighting troops?'

'A little.'

'How's it looking?'

The fellow didn't seem terribly communicative. He gestured again: 'Pretty chaotic.'

'Details!'

'The Russians have got through. Anyone still standing is running for it.'

The Sergeant held out the cigarette packet: 'Here, keep the pack.'

'Thanks.' He grew more talkative: 'There's already talk of them moving the Front back to the rail crossing-point. No idea where that is.'

'Left of the hill.'

'Never heard of it.'

'This road goes to Podrova. Things are going to get pretty hot around here . . .'

'Road!' The soldier shouldered his radio-pack again. 'It's a bloody forest path if you ask me.'

'Break a leg, eh!' said the Sergeant, and went on. Bit of luck, he thought. He felt a little more optimistic. He could stay on the road. With all the confusion, who could ever prove whether he had received orders or not? In Emga, he would join the baggage train. In fact, it was his duty to do just that. There'd be plenty for him to do. Collect up scattered groups of men. Double rations for the company. Maybe even chocolate. They would certainly need him there. Thoughtfully, he went on.

He never saw the soldier who was leaning casually against a tree. At most a shadow entered his unconscious.

'Sergeant!'

He turned with a start.

'Just a minute, please.'

The Sergeant saw the Corporal's stripes. 'What's got into you? Are you crazy?'

The Corporal walked calmly up to him: 'All right, where to?'

The Sergeant was bewildered: this had never happened to him before. He said: 'I won't be spoken to like that!'

He wanted to say more, but thought better of it. He walked resolutely on. The Corporal was holding him by the sleeve. Unexpectedly, he had seized hold of him.

'Goddamnit!' The Sergeant knocked the hand off his arm, less furious than bemused. Then he saw the tin badge on the Corporal's chest. He shut up. 'Well, about time,' said the Corporal with irritation. 'Military Police. Your documents please.'

The Sergeant grew unsure of himself. He had a feeling of foreboding in his stomach. As he opened his wallet, his hand shook. Hope he doesn't notice, he thought. 'You probably think I'm a spy or something,' he tried to joke. The Corporal looked him up and down while the Sergeant held out his pay-book as if it were a disappointing school report.

'Orders?'

'No orders.' He was amazed how calmly he said it.

'From where? Going where?' The Corporal kept staring into his eyes.

'My company is at the Front, by the side of the hill. I have to get to the supply column at Emga.' He was too agitated to consider what he was saying. What he said corresponded to an intention he had only recently thought of as perfectly acceptable. He couldn't think of anything better. He tried to calm himself, but still had a sensation of being garrotted.

'What's your business with the supply column?' The Corporal's voice had a strange undertone as he asked.

'As a Sergeant, my place is with the supply column.' This is crap, he thought in alarm.

'Not necessarily.'

The Sergeant started to cough. The Corporal waited politely till he had finished.

'At what time did you leave your company's position?'

Got to get this one right, he thought. The answer he gave now might be decisive. But everything in his head was a tangle. Shall I say: 'Before' or 'After'? 'Before' seemed better to him. But what about the intervening time? Suddenly he had the notion of running away. But the Corporal had a pistol, the holster was unbuttoned, the butt was sticking out. He abandoned the idea.

'At midnight,' he answered stoutly.

'You probably imagine we don't know what time the Russian bombardment began?'

What's that about? thought the Sergeant. He pondered. 'Well, of course, before,' he added.

'Exactly,' the Corporal remarked ironically. 'Why don't you come along with me.' He spun the Sergeant round, gave him a brusque shove in the back, and pushed him in front of him towards a clearing in the forest. The Sergeant involuntarily remembered the Russian prisoner. 'Human shield,' he thought. The night had begun with the push he had given the Russian; it would end with the push in his own back.

There was a jeep in the clearing. Only now did he notice the tracks on the forest floor. Why didn't I see them before, he wondered. Three MPs were leaning against it, smoking. Their steel helmets were lying in the grass. They looked up as he approached – a Lieutenant, a Sergeant, and an NCO.

'Well, Meyer, you demon, who have you come up with this time?' laughed the Lieutenant.

'Bit of a strange case, this one. Might be worth taking a bit of time over him.' The way the Corporal was speaking, it was as though there was no difference in rank between them. At least the Lieutenant's an approachable fellow, thought the Sergeant. He pulled himself together, to make a good impression. Stood up straight. Saluted.

'Lieutenant, beg to . . .'

'Ssh. Only speak when you're spoken to's how we do things here,' the Lieutenant said good-humouredly.

From behind, the Corporal reached into the Sergeant's inside pocket, pulled out his paybook, and handed it to the Lieutenant, who slowly began to leaf through it. 'Claims to have left his position at midnight. Confirms that the Russian bombardment had already begun. On his way to the supply column at Emga,' said the Corporal. He stressed 'midnight'.

'Why not just admit you've done a bunk,' said the Lieutenant equably.

'Lieutenant . . .'

'Yes or no. No stories.' A confusing manner he had.

'No, Lieutenant.'

'What were you doing for your company?' The Lieutenant straightened a creased page in the paybook.

'Platoon commander!' The Sergeant thought: Why did I write in all the details of what I was doing, and even get the Captain to confirm the dates?

'And so your commanding officer decides to send you back to supply in the middle of the bombardment, just before the onset of an enemy attack?'

The Sergeant chewed on his lip.

'It's my feeling,' the Lieutenant turned to the NCO, 'that we've got a live one here.'

The Corporal nodded: 'There's no reason for them all to be reservists.'

'Bad business,' the NCO threw in, obscurely.

The Sergeant felt sick.

'Well, let's be off then.' The Lieutenant stood up. 'Take him to Emga.'

'Yes, sir!' A hand took the Sergeant by the sleeve, and pulled him gently to the jeep. The Corporal got in behind the wheel.

'I want you back immediately!'

'Yes, sir!'

They rolled out of the clearing, and got on the road to Emga.

'Won't be so bad,' said the NCO, sitting next to him, and passed him a cigarette. So that the match didn't go out, the Corporal took his foot off the accelerator. The Sergeant pulled hard on his cigarette. 'You might be lucky,' said the NCO. The Corporal accelerated again. Funny, thought the Sergeant, they're making it sound as though I could be put

away for this business. He looked at the speedometer. The
needle was flickering around the 50 mark. A couple of times
they stopped for vehicles coming the other way. The Sergeant
received curious glances.

Emga. The road widened. Blockhouses. Up on a hill, a
church without a roof. A building on fire, to the right. The
jeep clattered over a rail crossing. Behind a steaming locomotive, a carriage with the windows whited out, and a large red
cross painted on the middle of it. Banners and signposts with
various tactical instructions rammed into the ground. In the
middle of the road, a fountaining explosion. Because of the
noise of the engine, the Sergeant had failed to hear the gurgling approach of the shell. He ducked. On the left, a long low
barrack hut. The divisional emblem stuck over the door,
skew-whiff. Soldiers carrying sets of files, loading them on to
lorries. Behind the low wooden fence, swaddled forms on
stretchers. The jeep stopped outside a tall barn. Plaster peeling off the outside. An MP standing outside.

'Come on, get a move on!' said the NCO, leaping out of
the jeep. 'Otherwise the Russian guns will get us!' He waited
impatiently for the Sergeant. The door was so low they had to
stoop. Inside, it was pretty dark. There was a cold draught.
The Sergeant couldn't see any windows in the barn, only a
little light came in through chinks in the walls. With practised
movements, an NCO with a bulldog's face took his pistol and
belt off him. He didn't have time to resist. Nor would there
have been any point. Sit tight. Talk to them later. He was
given a piece of card with a number on it. His name was
entered in a worn ledger. Then the NCO pushed him up a
staircase. Above them was a wire cage with a door in it. The
NCO unlocked a padlock, let the Sergeant step inside, and

clattered down the stairs. The Sergeant saw empty paper sacks. GERMAN PORTLAND CEMENT. All round damp brick walls. Three soldiers were sitting on wooden stumps, playing cards. Not cards, bits torn out of the paper sacks. Their uniforms dusty with cement. Overhead, beams and struts, and the undersides of red rooftiles. Feeble light came in through one or two chinks.

'The last trump!' The men paid no attention to his arrival. One of them spat on the floor. The Sergeant saw on his shoulder the traces of a removed Corporal's insignia. 'Maybe he can tell us what's going on! Hey, what time are the Russians coming?'

The Sergeant didn't answer.

'Shy?' They put together their bits of paper. Their laughter sounded edgy. 'Which commandment did you break? The eighth?'

'Save it,' said the Sergeant. Only now did he notice another figure squatting by the wall.

'Would the Sergeant be kind enough to let us know when the Russians are expected in Emga?' twitted the ex-Corporal. 'It's damned important for us.'

'And maybe for him as well,' said another.

A shell went up in the village. They listened. The Sergeant tried to work out which way the Front was. He couldn't do it. The soldiers went on taunting him:

'We're not good enough for him. A Sergeant finds it very hard to adjust.'

The Sergeant ignored them. He forced himself to be indifferent, contemplated the crumpled figure by the wall. He was boiling inside. It was just a misunderstanding. After all he'd gone back with the agreement of the Captain, had reported to

the Major, and was on his way to Emga, where else was there
to go anyway! Just a misunderstanding. Another crash outside. Dirt and splinters rattled on the roof, plaster dust
sprinkled down. Damnit, he thought, one can land here any
second, and we're sitting ducks. Just on account of a misunderstanding. He wanted to talk to an officer right away. Only
he needed to think about what he was going to say first. And
with this banter going on, he was unable to think straight.

'The gentleman can't have any information. Must have
come from the back area. Else he'd speak to us.'

'Shut up!' the Sergeant suddenly screamed.

They fell silent. Only for a moment or two. Then their
laughter burst in his face. The Corporal was bent double, as
though he had cramp. Behind it, though, was something dis-
concerting, fear and hatred. Abruptly, he stopped. A twisted
red face looked up at the Sergeant:

'You bastards brutalized us whenever you could. But not in
here, OK?' The veins in his temples stood out. Like a beast of
prey, he approached the Sergeant. 'I'm not going to make it
out of this rotten hole in my lifetime, and I don't care either.
But I've had enough, and I'm not going to take any more shit
from you or anyone!' His voice cracked. The Sergeant
flinched. The Corporal edged him back, step by step. A scar
gleamed on his forehead. The Sergeant groped his way along
the wall. The scarred forehead got closer and closer.

'Help! NCO!' shouted the Sergeant.

The Corporal's fist smashed into his face. He staggered.
From his throat came a gurgling sound. A second blow. He
didn't dare raise his hands. He sagged along the wall. Shut his
eyes. As though through a veil, came a sudden voice: 'Haven't
you had enough yet?' A whooshing sound. The Sergeant tried

to get his eyes to open. The MP was standing in the cell, whipping the man. Blow upon blow. Blindly whipping him about the head and shoulders. 'Stupid motherfucker!' The Corporal crumpled. The remaining prisoners pressed back into corners. The Sergeant felt satisfaction, and worked his boot into the Corporal's testicles. The MP spun round.

'Hey!' The NCO raised his whip.

The Sergeant jerked back. 'He punched me.' He felt a minuscule advantage as he sensed that the NCO didn't want to strike him.

'Shut up. You're all the same.'

'You'll be sorry you said that,' hissed the Sergeant. He bit his tongue. But the other looked at him in puzzlement. So that's the way to talk to him, thought the Sergeant. He ordered: 'Open the door! At once!'

'What?' said the NCO.

'I said open the door!'

Outside, an explosion hit very close to the barn. Plaster leaped out of the walls. A surge of air seemed to lift the roof. For an instant it was as bright as day. Rooftiles came clattering down.

By this time the Sergeant had calmed down, the MP had already stumbled down the stairs. A feeling of disagreeable sobriety remained in his wake. Spots of sun lit the floor, which was sprinkled with cement and scraps of tiles. The two prisoners got up, and dragged the Corporal into the shadows. They were like ruffled vultures, hunkering in a ruin after a failed expedition. Furious looks flew after the Sergeant.

The Sergeant was looking round anxiously. He stopped and looked at the man, who, during the altercation, had not moved. He was leaning against the wall, little more than a boy, terribly young. The uniform drooped off his narrow shoulders. Two bony hands, and a head that seemed much too heavy for the body. Under greasy hair, two shining, deep-set eyes. Awkwardly, the Sergeant seated himself at his side, in the lee of the wall. The cool, and the dimmed light, both calmed him.

'Are you not well?' he asked in such a quiet voice that the soldier barely understood the question.

The boy faintly shook his head. His eyes were directed at a particular spot, a white splotch of plaster on the opposite wall.

'How long have you been here?' the Sergeant asked softly.

'I don't know!'

'Surely you must know!'

Silence again. Then: 'They take me with them wherever they go. It's been a long time already.'

The Sergeant was startled. He had never seen such eyes. The dullness of a blind man lay in them. And yet they moved, took in his shoulder tabs.

'You're a Sergeant . . .'

'Yes. Have you received your sentence?' Maybe he might hear something that came in handy.

'Not yet,' said the boy.

'But you're waiting to hear?'

'Yes.' The boy looked dully, eyes front. The other three were watching them.

'And what did you do?'

'I hid.'

The Sergeant whispered: 'Hid?'

'We were to storm the Russian trenches, and I hid. On account of my mother.'

The Sergeant was disappointed. Fear would have been another matter. 'Your mother?' he asked, indifferently.

'She's alone, and I'm all she has in the world. Can you understand that?'

The Sergeant looked at the scrawny body, the bony fingers, the yellow skin pulled across the cheekbones. Suddenly he said: 'Well, I'm sure you'll never see your mother again!'

'That's all in God's hands,' the boy replied quietly.

'What God do you mean?'

'That one.' He pointed to the floor. He meant the MP.

'He's not a god!' The Sergeant pulled a face.

'We're all in his hands!' The boy's eyes started to flutter. The Sergeant felt a bit peculiar. He moved away.

'Idiot!' someone said on the other side.

'You'll see!' The boy's voice rang through the barn. The Sergeant shuddered.

'Have you got the time?' one of the three men asked.

Almost gratefully, the Sergeant replied: 'Eight.'

'So the day's just beginning then.'

7

'Achtung! Achtung! Calling all men. Between 0801 and 0810, we will transmit the time in clear,' a voice said in a forest, way behind the Front, into the microphone of a short-wave radio. The signals ran through spools and tubes and coils, clambered up a pole on a copper wire, and passed into the ether via an antenna. 'Achtung! Achtung! Calling all . . .'

'The army's broadcasting the time,' said an officer in the radio car of the divisional command. 'Tune to receive! Interrupt all messages!' The radio operators threw switches, twiddled knobs: synchronize watches. They passed on the incoming voice on whatever frequency they were on.

'. . . the time in clear,' heard the radio man in Podrova. He glanced down at his watch. They'll be transmitting that for the next nine minutes, he thought. Better if they listened to me. To what I've got to say:

. . . location podrova eastern exit road – lost contact with unit – enemy trench mortar fire on podrova – withdrawal to road – disorderly – elements of infantry, artillery, ack-ack – no weapons, no vehicles, no officers – no intact units – leaderless troops of men – wounded officer describes russian pincer movement on hill 308 – hill presumably still in our hands – end of message.

Instead of which the voice in his receiver said 'one minute past eight' and kept the wavelength occupied.

'Two minutes past eight,' heard the wireless operator at the five-way crossroads. He didn't have time to check his watch. Nor did he interrupt his transmission. Every radio operative within a radius of four kilometres heard his report, along with the time:

'This is saturn – waiting vainly for promised arrival of reserve battalion – in front of us russian tanks – not possible to tell numbers – defence collapsed – enemy breakthrough on a wide front to the north of own position – resistance of own troops in hollow – on hill 308 two enemy tanks no infantry – further resistance here impossible owing lack of ammunition – dynamiting radio – end of report! end! end!'

'Three minutes past eight,' he still heard. Then his radio exploded into the air like a champagne cork.

The Major wiped the mud off his watch. Four minutes past eight. So he'd been in the swamp for an hour. Up to his knees in water, and twice in it up to his chest. Lost a boot. His pistol clogged with mud. Compass broken. Both shoulder tabs torn off by branches. He looked like a wild animal. On, on, he thought. His hands were bleeding. Already he could hear the machine gun. Maybe three hundred yards more, and he would be with them . . .

The Lieutenant in one of the Russian tanks on the hill was

twiddling with his radio: 'Five minutes past eight,' a German voice said in his headphones. He didn't know any German. He watched the Siberians through the vision slits. They had rolled up part of the German trench, and now they were caught in a trap. There were thirty Germans in a defensive hedgehog at the foot of the hill, and they controlled the entire stretch. On the other side of the swamp, other Russian tanks were wheeling around. Each time the infantry came out from behind them they were caught in German machine-gun fire and mown down. He looked at his watch. The situation was getting unbearable. Three hours up on the hill already. His munitions cases were empty. Why didn't the carriers come and lay down a new carpet? His own artillery was shelling the heights. The splinters were pinging against his steel walls. He couldn't even climb out. For the past hour, he'd been parked next to the pylon with his engine off. He couldn't stick around here for ever. The hole under the concrete pediment had the look of an entrance. There was a battered tin can on the lip. All that kept him from climbing out and having a look was the mortar fire from his own side.

'Six minutes past eight,' came the German voice in his headphones, which he didn't understand.

Six minutes past eight, the NCO established. Cautiously he pushed his head over the earthworks. The sun was reflected in the puddles in front of the trench; behind the shot-up barbed wire were the silhouettes of Russian tanks. Brown cadavers all over the shop. Contorted limbs pointing up at the sky. A shot whistled by from his own trench. It splashed back from the tank turret. Crazy bastard, he thought, the guy's trying to shoot through the observation-slit.

'Forget it!' he shouted back along the trench. 'Otherwise they'll let us have it!'

The Runner came out from his niche and propped himself against the opposite trench-wall. He waved his fist in the air: 'What are they waiting for?' Right and left of the pylon sat the two tanks, and didn't budge.

'The anti-tank squad is fucked!'

'Yes, or they've fucked off!' The Runner spat into the trench. 'The bastards have fucked off out of it!'

There was some movement behind the tanks on the edge of the swamp. The NCO peered across.

'We ought to roll up the sap as far as the officers' dugout, then we'd have some air!'

The NCO didn't reply. A Red Army man leaped out from behind one tank, and scurried to the next.

'They've given up on us!' The Runner looked up into the sky. 'They won't even send us any air support!'

The Russian soldier over by the tanks ran past the shredded wire-entanglements. The enamel mess kit flashed against his hip. He waved his arms.

'I just had to get out of the wounded shelter,' explained the Runner. 'They were driving me nuts!'

Over by the wire, at the last of the tanks, the Russian suddenly stopped and ran back.

'Maybe it's best . . .' the Runner finished after a short pause, 'we just surrender?'

'Maybe?' The NCO glanced at him. 'If we knew what would happen to us . . .' There was a sudden surge behind the tanks. 'They're coming!' he yelled. The Runner leaped back into his hole. The two machine guns left and right started clattering away.

The NCO thought: they're attacking every half-hour. Involuntarily he looked down at his watch: it was seven minutes past eight.

Eight minutes past eight. The Russian Colonel nervously ran his ruler across the map spread out on the table.

'Unfortunately!' His Adjutant raised his shoulders inquiringly. He said: 'After the third tank, the carpet across the swamp broke up. The infantry is stuck. That was the end.' He pointed to a black-ringed number on the map: 'Zostchenko's battalion is in a fix!'

A draught picked up the map. The door had opened.

'How high are the losses?' The Colonel turned to look out of the window. A girl was standing on the street, with her hair blowing in the wind.

'So far,' said the Adjutant, 'we have no information.' He listened. The General's voice was heard from next door.

'Who is that person again?' The Colonel pointed out of the window at the girl.

'What person?' The Adjutant purposely looked past the girl.

Reproachfully the Colonel said: 'I mean who she goes with!'

'That's Zostchenko's girl!'

The Colonel nodded: 'All I know is, a dressing-station has called in extra help.'

'Yes, Comrade Colonel.'

The Corporal pushed the detonator into the bomb. It was quiet in their hole. He could hear the detonator grate against the metal wall of the bomb. He couldn't make out the hand or the numbers on his watch. The luminescence of the phosphorus was all used up.

'What are you doing?' asked a voice in the dark. 'We don't want to pay with our lives for your initiative.'

'Every one is free to do what he wants,' replied the Corporal. 'For instance, I am now going to blow up a Russian tank!'

The voice said: 'There are two of them. Then the other one will blow us . . .'

'Don't talk nonsense.' Once again, the scrape of the detonator against the metal.

'You're not going to!' said the voice, trembling.

The Corporal replied coolly: 'I've spent an hour thinking about it!' Avoiding any sound, he pulled up his legs, and shoved his back slowly up against the wall. The bomb was heavy.

There was movement opposite him. A hand reached for his arm. He hit it, hard. Two hands reached for his shoulders. He pulled up his knee, and lashed out with it. A groan of pain. Bad breath stank in his face. Already, he was propelling himself towards the way out. Held the bomb in his right hand, tried to pull himself up out of the hole with his left. Only now did he realize that his joints were stiff, and he had almost no strength in them. And the daylight was dazzling him too.

'You're crazy! Stay here!' shouted the desperate voice behind him.

Already his head was protruding out of the hole. And then someone grabbed his feet. An iron pincer held them. He had to free himself. Five steps in front of him loomed the clay-encrusted front of the tank. A monstrous track, screw-heads, welded seams. He fought hard. Tried to lift the bomb out of the hole, to roll it in the direction of the tank. The hands gripped him like a vice. His strength ebbed. 'Let me go,' he whimpered. The bomb pressed against his chest, so that he couldn't breathe. A little lid opened in the wall of the tank. A tube, like the spout of a watering can, pointed at his head. With the last of his strength, he pulled the safety catch.

At that moment, an oily fluid dripped out of the tube of the flame-thrower. A little spark flashed up. Suddenly an inferno squirted in his face. His head burned like tinder. The bomb began to glow. A mighty explosion: there was no more Corporal. A wave of pressure hissed into the hole. Air pushed against earth walls, against concrete, little spurts of flame raced in the direction of the remaining bombs. In no time, paper, uniforms, flesh were carbonized. The ignited explosive lifted the concrete lump, launched the skeleton of the mast into the air.

The Lieutenant in the tank heard the foreign voice once more. Then his turret began to spin with him inside it. The steel hull burst asunder. He didn't hear the voice make its last announcement: 'Ten minutes past eight.'

Somewhere, far behind the Front, a hand threw a switch. Little lamps went out. Wires cooled. From the East, new signals went on their complicated journeys.

8

Three movements saved the lives of the Captain and the wounded man in the shelter. Not for good, but certainly for some time. The Captain didn't have time to think about whether he was doing the right thing or not. He acted out of instinct. He picked up a stone, wrapped his dirty but still somewhat white handkerchief round it, and tossed it at the feet of the Red Army man who had suddenly materialized at the shelter entrance.

The lives of the two men at that moment depended purely on chance. A man who has covered three hundred yards of open ground through machine-gun fire and amid exploding hand-grenades, and then run through a labyrinth of unfamiliar trenches, and finished up standing in front of an enemy dugout with a grenade in his hand primed to go off in three seconds, is more in the nature of a machine. He might not see a white handkerchief wrapped around a stone. Or he might see it and think nothing of it. He might be in a sort of bloodlust. Or again, he might immediately realize what it means and still throw his grenade into the dugout, because he doesn't know what else to do with it. It was pure chance that the Russian threw his grenade over the rim of the trench. And everything that followed from that was, likewise, pure chance. In particular the fact that the Captain now found himself sitting as a prisoner in his own dugout.

The Captain didn't know how long it had been. His watch had disappeared along with various other items. It had to be hours. His nervousness had abated. He even felt a kind of calm. The critical point seemed to have passed. From experience he knew that prisoners are mostly shot during initial confusion. At least in his company, that was how it was. And these Russian soldiers didn't seem that different from his own men. Just different uniforms and other face-shapes. Apart from that, they were equally filthy, equally over-strained, and equally obedient. He was unable to ascertain who was commanding them, but there was a purpose in what they were doing. They searched his dugout, distributed what bread they found, checked their weapons, made room for the wounded men that others carried in, and tended to the wounded man from his company as if he was one of their own. He was almost in awe of their discipline. They were in the middle of a battle, and still they were at pains not to show it. He almost envied the wounded man, on whom they lavished more attention than they did on himself. He lay on the pallet between two Russians, with a rolled-up coat for a pillow, and covered with a canvas groundsheet. His arm was properly bandaged. They had got hold of some chocolate from somewhere, and brought some to their comrades, and gave the German a little bit as well. Tallow candles were burning everywhere, that they had brought with them. They smelled quite strongly, but every last corner of the dugout was lit up.

And yet – he had a feeling of something not quite right. There was still shooting in the trench, even though the artillery was quiet. A machine gun was clattering away. Further to the front, hand-grenades were going off. Nor were they taking any steps to remove himself or his comrade. That unsettled him. He was already quite reconciled to his destiny. In his imagination, he could see a barrack camp, barbed wire, and, for the first time in months, peace and quiet. No explosions, no shell craters, no orders, no responsibility. Thinking about it soothed him. He might have to wait a long time to be free, but even now he decided not to let himself get impatient. He could always learn the language, and study something interesting. He remembered lectures he had given to his secondary school pupils about the diverse peoples of the East. He began to engage with peaceful subjects once more. Already, he was far removed from his immediate situation.

'Hello,' a low voice said next to him. He turned in alarm, and found himself looking into an unfamiliar face. It struck him that the voice had spoken in German. They must have that just like we do, there's always someone who knows one or two words.

'Lieutenant Trupikov.' And the Russian bowed.

The Captain was so astonished, he instinctively stood.

'Please don't trouble yourself,' said the other with consummate politeness. He gestured towards a bench behind the rickety table made of ammunition crates. The Captain sat down in some confusion.

'Our battalion had the honour of storming your position. Unfortunately not wholly successfully. As you must have realized yourself.' The Russian took a tallow candle that was perched on a bayonet driven into the wall, and set it down on the table. He had strikingly fine and well-manicured hands. 'Cigarette?' He pulled out a cigarette case, flicked it open, and extended it across the table.

'Thank you.'

With two fingers, the Captain plucked out a cigarette. There was a German dog tag in the case. He shrank when he saw it.

'From one of your men,' the Russian said. And continued smoothly. 'I would like some information from you.' He paused. 'Of course, you don't need to reply if you'd rather not.' He smiled, and looked into the Captain's face.

The Captain hesitated. A minute ago, he would have been ready to give any information required of him. He was a prisoner, and his first thoughts were for himself. To a Sergeant, he would have capitulated. But now? He was confused by this Lieutenant. Now, he had better fight on, with different weapons. His personal dignity was at stake.

'I am in your hands,' he said, with as much calm as he could muster.

'This isn't to be an interrogation. Just a private question really.' The Russian fixed the decorations on the Captain's chest. 'Why do your men put up such desperate resistance?'

'But surely they're not resisting any more,' replied the Captain. The way the Russian was looking at him irritated him.

'They are.' The Lieutenant smiled. 'They're fighting like fiends. In the fighting trench, there's a troop of them that are surrounded but they still won't surrender. I should like to know why!'

So that's why there's still shooting going on, thought the

Captain. 'Which is the sector in question?' he asked. He wondered which it might be.

'Hard to describe,' said the Russian. He reached into a canvas bag on the bench next to him, and pulled out a pencil and paper. The smile about his lips disappeared. 'If this is the position . . .' He scrawled a line across the page, '. . . and this is the sap to your dugout, then it would be round about here . . .' He indicated a point along the line.

'Between the saps, then?' asked the Captain.

'Oh, there's another sap then!' The Russian drew a third line.

'And there's a connecting piece there,' said the Captain, 'and a deep dugout.'

'Hm.' The Russian looked up quickly. 'So that's where there's a troop from your company, refusing to give up.'

'Is their position hopeless?' The Captain stared abstractedly at the sketch.

'Yes. We're already established west of the hill. I'm pretty certain your men must realize that. But they're continuing to fight. I find it baffling.' Trupikov thought of the two tanks that only fifteen minutes ago had been blown up, along with the lump of concrete, and the bones of the pylon. He knew that the heights were once again no man's land. Before long, a German machine gun would open up there.

'My company consists of simple folk. Any leadership will avail itself of . . . propaganda methods. Do you understand? It's not easy for the men.' The Captain avoided looking at his captor. He stared instead into the candle flame.

'You mean – they're afraid of being taken prisoner?'

'Yes. It's possible they take an unduly pessimistic view of their prospects.'

'I understand.' The Lieutenant smiled. 'Among us, they say the Germans eat a lot of sauerkraut. When I went to Germany, I was curious. But I can set your mind at rest. You don't eat any more sauerkraut than we do.'

'You know Germany?' asked the Captain in surprise.

'I play the violin. I studied there.'

'Ah – so that's why!' And the Captain glanced at the well cared-for hands of the Russian.

'Will you excuse me a moment.' As Trupikov got to his feet, he asked: 'You don't know any Russian, do you?'

'No.'

The Lieutenant went outside, and issued some orders in Russian. The Captain noted to his chagrin that he had taken the sketch of the German position with him. He felt abandoned and forsaken. More unsettling than the inadequate connection with God was the sudden absence of a superior authority.

'I always felt very much at home in Germany,' said the Lieutenant, as though seeking to re-establish the cosy atmosphere by the mere fact of his return. But his face looked curiously tense: 'This will interest you. It seems a single man came out of the swamp, ran straight through my lines, and joined the little group of men surrounded in the trench.'

'Must have lost his way.' The Captain shook his head.

'He came from the rear – or from the front,' the Russian went on. 'Whichever way you want to put it. He vanished before my men could . . .' He corrected himself: 'Before my men could do anything to prevent him.'

'Soldiers are apt to get a little disorientated,' said the Captain. He thought: Here we are, two colleagues, teaching the same subject.

'True,' said the Lieutenant, 'but what shall I do if your soldiers refuse to surrender? I feel the prickings of conscience. That's what you say, isn't it?'

'Why?' The Captain thought about military academy: a cool exchange of ideas in front of the sandbox.

'We can't allow ourselves to be held up by them for ever,' said the Lieutenant. 'If they don't come to their senses . . .'

'Then what will you do?' A Captain testing the resolve of his Lieutenants in front of the sandbox.

Trupikov swiftly countered: 'I hoped you would have a suggestion for me.'

'Me?' The Captain felt imprisoned all over again.

'You could explain the situation to your soldiers. After all, lives are at stake.' Trupikov looked the Captain solemnly in the eye.

The Captain lowered his eye and looked off into the tiny flame of the candle. 'How – how would you view that?'

'I give you my word as an officer – if I was in your position, that's what I would do.'

'And what's your plan?'

'Very simple. We move you within shouting distance of your soldiers. You call on them to surrender and tell them I guarantee they will have honourable treatment.'

'I am an officer,' said the Captain. 'But – I'll do it.' He stood up.

'In case you misunderstand,' said the Lieutenant politely, and drew his pistol. They went outside.

The Captain was dazzled by the daylight. It was early morning. The trench looked devastated. They trod on corpses. The Captain saw what the artillery bombardment had done to his position. An earthquake had passed over the trenches, and only the deep dugout had survived it.

'Bend down,' ordered the Lieutenant.

He bent down. A bullet puffed up earth from the edge of the parapet. He was surrounded by Red Army men, all staring at him. When the trench straightened, he caught a view of the hill: a great bald place, shimmering in the sun. There were little clouds of smoke hanging over the earth. Perhaps some of his own trench mortars, trying to cut off the Russian breakthrough. They curved forward. The Red Army soldiers were carrying back a wounded comrade. They were sweating, and smelled of musk. The way up to the fighting trench had never seemed so long to the Captain. The pistol which Trupikov kept pointed at his back protected him from the aggression of the others. They reached the remains of the tank. The jagged hole punched in its side was like the mouth of a shark grinning at him. And here, there had been a direct hit. The trench widened out to a roundabout. In the middle lay a German soldier, slumped forward, his hands over his head. The Captain bent down over him. He saw the ragged scorched hole in his neck where he'd been shot.

The Lieutenant angrily ordered him: 'Keep moving!'

They reached the firing-trench. Shredded bodies in German uniforms. Dried puddles of blood. A disfigured face, without any body. The ravaged machine-gun emplacement. The machine gun was gone. More Red Army guards. They reached the furthest point where they had protection from German fire. Beside them was a Russian machine gun, loosing off sudden bursts along the trench. Behind a low earthwork, squeezed together, four Russians staring ahead.

'Here!' said Trupikov, and threw himself on the ground. 'Here we're in hand-grenade range!'

The alarmed Captain sank down beside him.

'Go on. Begin,' said Trupikov. He spat. A bullet fizzed over his head.

'Hello, comrades!' shouted the Captain.

'Louder,' said Trupikov.

The Captain cupped his hands round his mouth: 'Comrades!!'

A stalk with a dark head came whirling through the air, and splashed into a puddle in front of them. The next instant came the bark of an explosion.

'Your men are suspicious of you,' said Trupikov.

The Captain called out: 'This is your company commander speaking to you! Can you hear me?' A hail of machine-gun bullets kicked earth in his face. 'Please, be sensible!' He shouted out excitably: 'It's me, Captain Waldmüller!'

Finally there was quiet. A hate-filled voice called out: 'It's all a trick, Comrade Ivan! We know you!' The Captain tried to identify the angry voice. It didn't sound familiar to him. 'Is that you, Lutz?' he asked.

'He's dead! I expect you found his paybook!'

'No, it's me! Waldmüller!' He shouted in despair: 'Please believe me!'

There was silence for thirty seconds. They seemed to be consulting.

Then a voice called out: 'What's our CO called?!'

'Major Schnitzer!'

'And the Runner?!'

It was still the same voice which he couldn't identify. 'Braun!' he called.

'And what do you want from us?'

'I'm a captive. I've been put in the picture.' The Captain

lifted his head. 'Your resistance is futile. If you don't surrender . . .' He looked in Lieutenant Trupikov's direction.
Trupikov nodded. 'You've nothing to be afraid of. You'll be
well treated!'

He stopped and waited.

'Captain?'

'Yes?'

'Why is our resistance futile?'

'You're surrounded! The Russians are already in Emga!'
He caught an approving nod from the Lieutenant, and realized too late that he hadn't stuck to the truth. He started to
sweat.

'Wait a minute,' he heard someone call. After a time came
the question:

'Waldmüller! Are they threatening you?'

The voice seemed familiar. One more sentence and he'd be
able to place it.

'No,' he called back.

'Waldmüller, don't talk nonsense! I know you're not talking
freely!'

The Captain was startled. He had made out the Major's
voice. How did he come to be in the trench? The Major was
supposed to be in Podrova. He looked imploringly at the
Russian and said vaguely: 'I just want to stop further blood-
shed.'

'Waldmüller,' shouted the Major, 'if they're threatening
you – we've got a Russian Captain here. I'm prepared to
exchange captives.'

'I'm not being threatened!' the Captain shouted promptly.
He mopped his brow. His hand was soaked.

'Find out his name,' said Trupikov quietly.

'What's the Captain called?'

'We don't know. He's with the platoon that are holding you.'

'Zostchenko,' murmured the Lieutenant.

'The officer's wounded. Negotiate an exchange. You against the Russian!' called the Major.

The Captain was in despair. Peace, which had beckoned to him moments ago, was already receding into the distance.

'Surrender,' ordered Trupikov angrily.

'The Russians won't accept your suggestion!' called the Captain with relief. 'It's futile anyway. I advise you . . .'

'Waldmüller! I hear you . . .'

'Major!' He no longer had any idea how he might persuade him.

'Can't understand,' he heard the Major say. Abruptly he asked: 'By the way, Waldmüller, have you given the Russians the secret of the dugout?'

'Major . . .' The Captain remembered the sketch. His hands were shaking.

'I want an answer!'

Lieutenant Trupikov inspected his pistol with interest.

'Major!' cried the Captain, at his wits' end. 'Talk it over with the men!'

'That's all, Waldmüller. You have my sympathy. Enough.'

The Lieutenant smiled: 'Come.' They made to stand up, but immediately bullets whistled past their ears, and they had to crawl back. German bullets, thought the Captain. Did God really not want to do a deal?

9

Sonia Shalyeva was running along a hollow. The air smelled of gunpowder. The grass on either side was burned, and at the deepest point of the dip she saw a dead man. He lay right across the path. His bandaged arms were pointed up at the sky. He had fallen off the back of a lorry. Not one of the soldiers rushing past had paid him any attention. In spite of her quilted uniform, which was too thick for the warm morning, she felt a shudder.

Beyond the slope, the path crossed a railway line. Some Red Guards carried on down the path, others turned right or left and went along the tracks. She asked for directions to the dressing-station to which she had been detailed. A commissar pointed down the tracks, turned and rushed on his way.

She walked over railway ties for a while, and asked a Red Guard if this was the way to the hill. The man told her she was almost there. There was shelling in the woods, and she walked faster. A group of Cossacks came riding along the rails. They yelled something she didn't understand, and cracked their whips in the air. Runners passed her, and wounded men tottered to the rear. The earth shook with the detonations. There was drumfire over the German front.

Gradually, the distance between the rail ties grew too great for her stride, and she was forced to walk on the sharp ballast stones. Her feet started to burn. But the line seemed unending. Finally, she reached a clearing, a green meadow pocked with black craters. The blockhouse there was the dressing-station she had been told to report to. All round stood Red Guards in white bandages. Some were lying quietly on the grass, others were groaning and crying. She saw grey colourless faces, and filth-encrusted uniforms. Sweat poured down her face, and her hair dropped into her eyes. She made her way across to them, with a little difficulty. She mustn't show any weakness. When she recognized one of the Siberians, she asked him: 'Have you seen Captain Zostchenko?'

'No.' The man was lying in the grass, facing the sky. Blood ran over his lips.

She asked aloud: 'Is there anyone else here from Zostchenko's battalion?'

Six said they were.

'Have you seen the Captain?'

'If you had some water for me, Comrade!'

'Have you seen the Captain?'

'No!'

'No . . . no . . . I think . . .'

She was ashamed of her questions, and turned towards the house. Maybe someone in there would know something.

When she opened the door, she found herself staring into a slaughterhouse. She felt she was choking, and unable to move. A doctor in a bloodied apron came up to her.

'Comrade, I've been waiting for you for an hour. At last a woman's hand!' He pushed an apron into her arms.

In a toneless voice, she asked: 'Do you have any news of Captain Zostchenko?'

'Please . . . don't make any difficulties, comrade. I need you urgently!' He simply tied the apron on to her.

She saw a table covered with an oilcloth. Instruments glittered in a bucket.

'Next!' He didn't even give her a moment to look around. Rough hands hoisted a body on to the table.

'I'd be happy if you just held their hands,' said the doctor. 'Just the mere presence of a woman works wonders.'

She reached for the wounded man. The soldier had a blood-soaked bandage round his head. A medical orderly peeled it off him like peeling a fruit. The dried blood tore like paper. She stood at the head end of the table, and found herself staring at a pulsing white mass.

'Do you see the splinter?' asked the doctor.

She didn't see anything. Only blood and brains.

A silver needle prodded into the jelly. It puffed up, and collapsed again. She felt sick.

'I've got it,' said a faraway-sounding voice. She closed her eyes.

'That'll do.'

By the time she opened her eyes again, the orderly was putting on a fresh bandage. Let me go, she wanted to ask. But her voice failed. The room started to spin. She planted her feet apart on the ground.

'Next!'

The next man had no hands.

'Take his head!' ordered the doctor.

This time she shut her eyes right away. She tried to picture Zostchenko. The stable light flickering. The horse whinnying. 'He's gone,' he said. She opened her eyes in alarm.

'I said he's gone!' the doctor turned impatiently to the orderly. The man was no longer breathing.

'Next!'

'Are you wounded?' asked the doctor.

'I'm sick!'

'Sick?'

The orderly said: 'He hasn't even got a temperature!'

'Has he got a temperature, comrade nurse?'

She laid her hand on the soldier's brow. She thought: he's feverish, I'm feverish, we're all feverish. The soldier was still young, and she looked into his eyes.

'You must rejoin your unit. You must go back to Captain Zostchenko.' And she said: 'He needs every man.'

'Yes, comrade!' The soldier turned over, and reeled away, as though drunk.

'Next!' said the doctor, tired.

She wanted to swap places. If she'd been on the other side of the table, she would have been able to look out of the window. But she couldn't move. The floor was covered with wounded men. The only space was on her side. She stared at the oilcloth. The soldier on the table had a jaunty little moustache, and he was drunk.

'I can't feel anything,' he said cheekily.

The orderly pulled off the bloodstained trousers. He looked in alarm at his superior, and then across to her.

'Bandage him, quickly,' said the doctor.

'What's the matter?' the wounded man asked. Before she could do anything to prevent it, he had pulled himself upright.

An animal scream came out of his mouth as he saw the wound. His feet drummed on the table. He raged, roared, wept. His spittle foamed. Then he suddenly collapsed. His features relaxed. He seemed years older. The moustache looked false. He wouldn't try it on with a woman again. He passively allowed himself to be bandaged up and carried outside.

'Next!'

They pushed him on to the table like a board. He lay wrapped in a canvas sheet. Under the sheet, his body reached only as far as his upper thighs. The orderly moved the bucket with the tools to the place where his feet should have been.

When she saw what they were about to do, she looked away. Once again, her thoughts concentrated on Zostchenko. It was the little attic room in Leningrad. He was sitting next to her, stroking her hand. She could feel his tenderness to her now. She felt a bitter surge of melancholy. They would never be together again like that. Life lay ahead of her like a grim road leading to a dump . . .

A shell came down in the clearing. The tools jingled together in the bucket. A saw was scraping.

'Now the other one,' said the doctor.

Another shell exploded. The earth shook. The beams ground together. Smoke came in through the open window, and the saw scratched on, as though nothing existed except this hut, and men with too many bones.

With the next shells, she heard the detonation. Two, three, four furious blows clawed at the house. The door was torn off its hinges. Smoke burst in. The soldiers outside, like animals, pressed in, looking for somewhere to shelter.

'Calm!' ordered the doctor, without stopping what he was

doing. A cat hopped on to the window sill. Its back arched. It was looking for the proximity of humans.

'Is his pulse still beating, Comrade Nurse?'

She couldn't feel anything. Only cold, bony hands. One of the thin fingers had a ring on it. More and more soldiers kept pushing into the room. They jolted each other, crowded round the table, and trod on the wounded men on the ground. Every one was seeking shelter under a roof that could no longer provide it.

The orderly shouted: 'Stay outside, you idiots!'

A deafening crash. Dazzling light pulsed through the room. The orderly was sent spinning. The saw stopped.

'Comrade Nurse!'

She only saw how everyone crouched. The cat jumped over the bodies on to the table. Dust particles whirled through the air, settled on the oilcloth, on her lips, on the tools in the bucket.

'Comrade Nurse, help the Sergeant!'

She let go of the icy hands, stooped to the bucket. A further rending crash. The table went over. Screams. Her hands groped into space. Her feet stepped on bodies, on faces. She plunged outside. The grass under her feet felt soft like cottonwool. The meadow was insanely green. She dropped under the nearest tree, and began to cry. Perhaps for Zostchenko. She felt she had abandoned him. She cried for herself, because she loved him.

10

Mortar shells had been bursting for half an hour in the trench by the foxhole and on the dugout of Schnitzer's surrounded platoon. They went up from the Red Army controlled sap outside the former company HQ, tipped at the apex of their flight like steel shuttlecocks, and exploded with eerie precision just at the entrance. There was no longer any dead ground, and the depth of the trench was no use: they were rats in a trap. It didn't seem possible that the Russians could have seen the deep dugout. There was nowhere from where one could see into it, and there were no bodies on the rim of it. A fiendish chance was directing the rifle-grenades, and Major Schnitzer thought he knew its name: it was Captain Waldmüller. In actual fact, though, it was the Russian hand-grenade which had been flung, not into the Captain's shelter, but over the perimeter of the trench. And there was something methodical about the operation of this chance. It had snuffed out Corporal Schute like a candle flame in the wind.

The Runner left the Corporal to lie where he was, and barricaded himself into the dugout. He left just a crack open.

That way he could see into the trench a little way. He pressed himself against the passage that led down into the foxhole, and peered out.

*The foxhole was proof of the fact that the blocking position had seen better days. One day when the combat engineers had relieved the trench platoon, they had found a sign: **Villa Foxhole**. If it had still been in its original place, it would almost have been a guarantee of quiet and security. But the manner in which it was found practically bespoke the opposite. The combat engineers saw that the trench was not very deep. They began to dig straight away, and saw that the labyrinth of the blocking position had simultaneously served as a mass grave. Under just a hand's breadth of soil, they started to encounter bodies. Their shovels bit into mouldering flesh, scraped bones, smashed through skeletons. By the light of flares, they encountered a skull with a Russian helmet adhering to it. A skeleton held together by a lichenous belt. Thousands of little flies swarmed through the trench. Whoever wasn't wearing a gasmask got lungfuls of putrescence. The blocking position had turned into a pit of pestilence. Ghostly shadows flung shovelfuls of stinking muck over the parapet like maniacs. They were like divers who had gone down into a sunken wreck, and stared at each other through its deadlights and portholes. The mass grave had three distinct layers. The engineers had to wear gloves where they couldn't reach with their shovels. And in between these layers, someone found the half-rotted piece of wood bearing the legend **VILLA FOXHOLE**. Written by one of the bony hands that had been shovelled over the parapet. So there must have been days here when they had leaned against the trench walls with their shirts off, smoked cigarettes, talked about leave, and lit fires against the midges. But that was a while ago.*

★

The passage where the Runner was now lying was a runnel cut diagonally into the ground. Narrow as a sewage pipe, and dark and damp. At the end was an entrance with a real wood door. A big lid off a chest, hung on leather hinges, and with **Army Property! This way up!** written on it. And behind the door, an anteroom. Incredible luxury. Perhaps an airlock. It was too narrow to serve for accommodation. But it was panelled with pine boards, and even lined with newspaper. If you were bored, you could read that the German armies were continuing their advance east, that Herr Maier had slipped away peacefully in his sleep, that eggs would be distributed again on Monday. But that must be a hundred years ago. The accommodation room was behind a further lid. There was room here for an entire platoon, but it was too low to stand up in. On the floor there was something that must once have been hay. Muddy boots and stagnant air had turned it to mouldering dung. On this dung there were now nine wounded men, among them Captain Zostchenko. Early that morning, there had been eleven. The Runner had lugged out the other two, and deposited them over the parapet. They had bled to death. From the living quarters, separated by a canvas sheet, there was an opening into the sleeping quarters. That had been wrecked by a direct hit from a shell. Twelve Russian soldiers had been taken in their sleep by the shell. It hadn't been possible to remove the bodies. The rubble couldn't be cleared, otherwise there was a chance the foxhole would have collapsed. No, right from the start, they hadn't had too many illusions about this position. Not the Captain, who was now in Russian hands in the company HQ. Not the Sergeant, who had done a bunk to Emga. Not the NCO who was manning the machine gun. And least of all himself, the

Runner. The shelter was like a dark tomb, filled with an infernal stench.

For that reason, and no other, the Runner had gone to lie in the passageway. If a rifle-grenade exploded at its mouth, he would turn his head away in a flash. It was still preferable to enduring the groans and cries of the wounded down in the hole. Outside the entrance, the dead Schute kept adding to his collection of shrapnel. Each time, he moved, and it looked as though he was still alive, or maybe being electrocuted. Now he waved with his hand, now he flipped over, and his dead eyes confronted the Runner, as though to say: Well, what do you say now? There wasn't really a whole lot you could say . . .

The pool in the Schutes' garden probably wouldn't get built now. Not unless Frau Schute married again, that is. She looked pretty young on the photo he'd seen of her. Her letter was in the dead man's breast pocket. It was only a week old, and had already suffered from a bit of shrapnel. Pretty harmless letter, really. He wasn't to worry about her, she was fine. Then something about the garden, about how hard it was to get a maid these days, and a room that mustn't be allowed to be left empty . . . The lodger was very nice. And then: there were a lot of stories these days about soldiers going off with girls. She was liberal in that regard, life was too short. A sensible woman, Frau Schute. Modern views. Perhaps even a tad too modern. Various points in the letter had not been clear to the recipient; he, the Runner, had had to read it too. He also claimed not quite to see what was going on. But there was another letter as well, that Schute didn't know about. 'Here, read this,' said the Battalion Adjutant. 'You decide if Schute should get this or not.' It was a neighbour writing with observations that people had made of Frau Schute's relationship with her lodger. And that was very clear. The Runner had looked at the Adjutant and shaken his head. In all probability, the business would take care of itself. And that's what had happened. A period of mourning, for public consumption. Firm, silent handshakes. Long faces. The lodger continued to be very nice. Life is short. Anyway. Hadn't Schute himself? . . . No? Well, never mind. Where his wife was so accommodating. There were girls everywhere. A soldier's life – a fun life! Big firework display on Hill 308. Commando raid against Russian bunker position. Corporal Schute right wingman. Green flares. Surprise firing. Machine-gun bursts. Run two hundred yards across open terrain. Hand-grenades. Life is short, Schute. Sure, with a strange man in the house, you're bound to get tongues wagging. Mine-laying at midnight. Schute responsible for activating them. Russian machine guns spraying no man's land. Use any available cover. With a live mine, your life is hanging by a thread anyway. You can be assured I'll be accommodating. 0610: attack. Concentric charge. Go on, Schute, get out of that trench. Heart pulsing in your neck, lungs bursting. On – under the bullets. Arm the fuses. A man who is exempt from active service. Alarm at dawn. The Russians are in front of our lines. Hand-grenades out! Too late, they're on us. Take the rifle-butt, the bayonet, the field-shovel. You must kill. For the sake of your wife, Schute! For a . . .

The Runner picked up a stone and flung it at the face of the dead Corporal Schute. And now he wanted to take another look at the puffy face down in the foxhole, with the buck teeth and the wound to the hip. He crawled backwards down the passage. He slithered over moist soil. Kicked open the chest-lid door. His hands groped in the darkness over the papered walls. Then he found the door to the main room. In front of him, in the dim candlelight, a gurgling bundle. The replacement with the horse face and the laid-open hip. The baker. Red-rimmed eyes looked at him.

'It seems the story you told was true after all,' the Runner growled maliciously to him. 'You slept with soldiers' wives and paid them with bread. You gave the local Commandant a car. You paid off the Mayor. You and your mill! But it was no good to you in the end.' The horse face looked at him in astonishment. 'You blabbed it all in your fever, you sonof-abitch!' The Runner yelled in triumph: 'Now you've got your just deserts. We're surrounded. You'll never get out of this shithole.'

He spat against the wall, and reeled out. He was deaf to the howls of the wounded. And to the mortar that could tear him in pieces any second. He didn't see the shellbursts, or dead Schute either. He took his rifle, and smashed the stock off it. He tossed the broken weapon into the foxhole, and pulled himself up the wall of the passage. Before he straightened up, he pulled his crumpled pass out of his pocket. Then he jumped up and ran. With arms aloft, and the scrap of paper in his right hand.

The Russian rifle fire stopped in surprise. He found himself at the centre of an eerie stillness. All he heard was his breath, the smacking sound of his boots when he trod in puddles. Suddenly he sank down. Any moment he was waiting for the whiplash of a gunshot, in front of him or behind him. Nothing happened. Only his boots got heavier. Every step took him closer to the line of swamp. He hadn't thought of that. The morass clung to his feet like lead. Impressions blurred in front of his eyes. Crazy faces started dancing in front of him: now it was the hill, now it was his two kids, holding out their hands to him, and finally a couple of fireballs.

His feet were up past the ankles in porridge. A few yards on, and it was calf-high. He lost one boot, then the other. Ran on barefooted. Waved the pink scrap of paper like a lunatic. The bandage started to come off his thumb, waved above him like a white flag. Finally the barbed wire. His uniform was shredded. His skin ripped, limbs ached. Dead Russians dangled in the barbed wire. Contorted faces under battered helmets. Now . . .

Now the shot had to come. From one side or the other. Why did it not come? As if they couldn't see him. Or were they all watching? Saw his cowardice, and reckoned he wasn't worth a bullet? The voice of the NCO: You coward! His own voice: I'm not a coward. A deserter, jeered the NCO. No one had called out. He was hearing things. The barbed wire was behind him. He dropped exhausted into a pit. Quaking with fear, he held out the pink slip to a pair of slitty eyes.

Two, three brown-clad forms launched themselves at him. Pinned him to the ground. Went through his pockets. Let him go. An unambiguous gesture gave him to understand he was to crawl on along the pit. A guard came after him. Above him, twittering bullets. From the German lines. At last he dared to stand up. The short tube of a trench mortar pointed to the sky. Hostile glances were directed at him. On the flat terrain, a tank, its gun pointing west. Soldiers hunkered down in the lee of it. No one paid any attention to the pink slip the Runner was still holding out in his hand. Even though he showed it to everyone he saw.

A leather-clad figure climbed out of the tank, jumped down beside him in the trench. The Commissar wore a pistol on a string around his neck. He went up to him, smacked him hard across the face. The blow burned his cheek. He felt miserable. He began to pant for breath, and his bare feet hurt him. He tried the might of the free pass once more. The man ripped it out of his hand, and trampled it into the mud. He felt he had lost his most valuable possession. The Commissar screamed at him, but he couldn't understand a word. More blows. Rough hands tore at his pockets. The photo of his children, the photo of his wife, torn in pieces and scattered over the ground. Tears came to the Runner's eyes. The Commissar spat in his face. He screamed out a command. One of the Red Guards grabbed him by the arm and dragged him away. Kicks lit into his back, a parting cuff knocked his head. He fell down. His hand groped for a shred of a photograph. He tumbled into a ditch after his guard. The ditch led back from the line. They tripped over dead Russians. One of them bore a resemblance to Corporal Schute, and suddenly all the others looked familiar as well. Pale and lifeless – a waxworks. Skin velvety like peach skin. The lips seemed to move. He saw a mocking, leering grin . . .

'Let me go,' he screamed in rage. His escort smashed him in the chest with a rifle butt. His last word turned into a gurgle. He tottered on. They came to the foot of a west-facing slope. Innumerable holes dug in it. The Runner was shoved into one of these. A group of Red Guards took him over. They led him along a passageway that had water dripping off the ceiling. Just like the foxhole, thought the Runner, only more extensive and damper. They came to a cave. He saw a wobbly table. The interrogation began. He stood barefoot in a puddle of water. A candle leaked wax on the table. He was falling over tired. A chill crept up his legs. A mild voice the other side of the candle asked questions. He couldn't make out the face, couldn't see through the trembling candle flame.

Behind it, everything melted into darkness, but he wasn't allowed to move. Beside his face a hand was toying with a pistol. When he didn't want to answer the first question, he felt a cold muzzle against his neck. The voice reeled off question after question. He had to answer fast, and without hesitation. If he hesitated, the pistol butt smashed him on the back of the head. They had surely broken his skull. He didn't know where the answers came from. They flew to him from somewhere. Company? Battalion? Commanding officer? Strength of the unit? Artillery positioned where? He answered every one. He wanted to add that he was a deserter; that it said on the pass that he would be well treated. The voice didn't give him the time to say any of that. It was an unfeeling machine that was confronting him. The chill from the puddle was creating an icy fire in his belly. His head ached with fever. Even his thumb began to hurt. He was swaying. The candle slid towards him, retreated. They had no pity. He was spouting nonsense. They beat him. Kicked him in the stomach. His knees were bleeding. His tongue licked across his gums. His teeth lay on the ground, hard pieces of dirt with blood on them. They kicked him in the testicles until he doubled up. As he fell, he whimpered for mercy. His vocal cords failed. With his hands he tried to convey that he was a deserter. They dragged him out to the exit. Rolled him down the steep slope. He somersaulted down. His battered face brushed the earth. A rock hit him on the forehead. He opened his eyes. They saw a new tormentor. He no longer felt the blows that pulled him to his feet and drove him forward. He tumbled through the ditch, past guns, equipment and Red Guards. They watched him pass, as if he'd come up from the Underworld. He spat blood. His ragged trousers were like a loincloth. Shreds of fabric clung to his bloodied filthy thighs. His legs quaked like steel rods. Sinew and bone. He ran in the sun. His shadow skipped after him like an imp. He was like a shy cave-dwelling beast that had lost its way in the daylight and was looking in dazzlement for somewhere to hide.

He would have fallen over a stretcher, had not his escort caught him by the arm. The Red Guard forced him to pick up one end. The other fellow, a Russian, he only ever saw the back of. They were carrying a casualty. His guard could no longer drive him forward, but the weight of the stretcher threatened to pull him down at any moment. He was as stiff as a piece of wood. Every step was a jab in the spine, every unevenness of the ground a burning pain in his chest. He pressed his smashed gums together. He had to cough. He spat. A gobbet of blood flew into the grass.

The wounded man on the stretcher stared up at him. He was terrified the battered specimen of humanity would drop him. Dimly the Runner saw the imploring eyes resting on him. Strange sounds clicked in his ears. Like a hammer striking tree trunks. When air-pressure swatted him aside, he saw the guns point their gaping maws to the heavens. He no longer heard. He was deaf.

At some spot swarming with men in white bandages, he was allowed to set down the stretcher. He was buffeted this way and that. Soldiers elbowed him aside. Red Guards, wearing the same filthy rags as he was. His own guard was lost in the crush. Strange sounds reached his ears as though through a fog. A white coat surfaced. Two hands carefully pulled off his tunic. A needle pierced his right upper arm. Immediately, a sweetish stream of warmth and serenity flowed into his veins. The drumming at the back of his head abated. His muscles relaxed. He sank to the ground with leaden exhaustion. He watched as someone bandaged up his thumb, daubed his gums with a styptic liquid. He was given a space on the grass, was covered with a coat that smelled of camphor, and sank in a sea of dull indifference. In the noisy confusion of the dressing-station, he thought he had finally found the best spot in the world.

11

The tide came from the forests at Podrova, streamed past the walls of the barn and burst crashing against the station at Emga. They were coming out of the dip behind the hill. From the swamps, from the crossroads, from all over, anywhere there were intact positions east of Emga in the dawn. As with any panic, the cause was relatively trivial: a herd of tanks that was slowly advancing along the tarmac from Podrova to Emga. The olive-green beasts had to proceed in single file on the narrow roadway. The machine gun of the lead tank drove hundreds of soldiers ahead of it, and broke loose everything that still wanted to adhere to organization and command structure: the healthy and the wounded, officers and men. Artillerymen abandoned their loaded pieces. Companies of untried reservists tossed their rifles away. They joined the fleeing mass stampede. The swamp kept spitting out more units, either side of the tarmac. An officer who tried to oppose the tide was simply dropped into the swamp. By the time he had freed himself of its sticky embrace, the human tide had already stampeded past. All that were left to him

were the last rows, where Death was reaping his harvest. Here
staggered the wounded and the weaklings. The machine gun
mowed them down like a scythe. The tail-end kept growing
back. There were always more.

At around noon, they reached Emga. They poured on to
the station platform. Threw themselves stupidly onto a train
without a locomotive. Hundreds fought over places in car-
riages that were not coupled together. Whoever had gained a
place defended it to the death. Rifle butts smashed down on
fingers that clung on to iron handholds. Kicks and punches
were dealt out. Fearful faces, imploring hands, burst-open
wounds. Hatred and enmity. Duels over standing room in
wagons with uncoupled chassis. The tracks swarmed with the
beaten-back, the desperate, the amputees and the feverish,
men with no hands to grab hold of anywhere. The train was
the destination for all of them. The train that wasn't a train.
The Fata Morgana on the siding. Wagons stood on blocks.
Wheels that could no longer turn.

The jeep speeding towards Emga only grazed the edge of the
chaos. The Judge Advocate sitting beside the driver watched
the panic impassively. He wasn't interested in troop movements. Undisciplined units, he thought. All he was interested
in was jurisprudence.

It wasn't until the main square in Emga that the driver
encountered any difficulties. The jeep was jammed tight. The
Colonel had to get out, had to force his way through troops to
get to Battalion HQ. The physical proximity of so many dirty
and unkempt men made the Colonel feel sick. With half-
closed eyes, he allowed himself to drift up to the HQ building.
What had necessitated his journey through this human sludge

was an order he had received to proceed to Emga and deliver sentence on a deserter. He was to report back to the army the instant the sentence had been carried out. He had known clearer orders. A deserter in Emga – which one?! Deliver a sentence – which sentence? This sort of thing required preparations, reports, meetings. The Colonel, a prosecuting counsel in civilian life, was used to the law. The law was always clear, it was lapidary, unambiguous sentences, each with its individual meaning. With this army command, the principal matter seemed to reside somewhere between the lines. Something in the order of: exceptional circumstances require exceptional measures. At least, so it appeared to him. He shivered a little, like a conscientious bookkeeper sitting in a drafty office. This wasn't his remit. He liked to go by the rules. These sort of insinuations were like black ice. Anyway, the order said he was to be responsible for the process. That meant legal process. Therefore, he had to obey. If need be, he could always appeal to that. Whatever might be between the lines was no affair of his.

Amidst all the confusion, the local headquarters was like a lifeboat in a flood. It was where all those assembled, with their guilty consciences, who had already left the sinking ship. Everyone tried to mask his personal failure with some sort of claim or complaint. But the local commandant, a fat little Major, had nothing, only forms. He ran around with a flushed face and plenty of responsibility. He listened to all kinds of stories. Very little of it, if any, was true. 'My battery needs ammunition, otherwise I can take no further responsibility for it!' The guns of that battery had been deserted next to the tarmac. The artillerymen were squabbling over seats in the ghost-train. It was widely known that headquarters had no

ammunition. 'If my unit doesn't get any more petrol, I shall
have to dynamite the vehicles!' The vehicles only existed on
paper. Fully laden with equipment and petrol for three days,
they were ablaze in the forest. The unit commander had personally torched the staff car. 'At least give me a jeep for the
dressing station! I've got to relocate!' The staff surgeon and
his limousine had sunk in the swamp. The man urgently
needed the jeep for himself. 'Require written confirmation
that my battalion is no longer combat-available . . . need
rations . . . cartridges . . . urgent replacements . . . regret,
without anti-tank weapons, impossible . . . can take no further
responsibility . . . can take no responsibility . . . no responsibility . . .' The Major, who for the past half-hour had also
been acting Commander-in-Chief at Emga, had heard this
sentence a hundred times already. In addition, there were the
sounds from outside, the engine noise of the Russian fighter
planes, the crash of ack-ack gunnery, the bleeping of tele-
phones. Luftwaffe Command: 'Where is the front line as of
this moment?' Army Corps: 'Special powers for acting C-in-
C at Emga!' Commissariat: 'Am making you personally
responsible for local supply situation.' Divisional command:
'Require situation report!' Those morons!

The Judge Advocate with rank of Colonel was forced to
chase the Major through his rooms, as he flitted here and
there like a weasel. The atmosphere was familiar to him.
When they recognized him – and they all recognized him –
then there followed the chill breath of his title, which he mis-
took for respect. It was almost like being at home:
apprehension, anxious waiting, furtive glances – just like what
he got as he strode through the halls of justice. Decked out in
gown and dignity, stepping confidently and nimbly from

paragraph to paragraph: the attorney-general. An obsequious greeting to him was required as part of the urge to survive . . .

They all greeted him. He was pleasantly aware of the fact that they bowed ever so slightly. Only the NCO of the Military Police remained stiff and upright. The effort of a court servant to appropriate some of the general attention to himself. In any case, order prevailed here. Maybe it wasn't so bad outside. Still, exceptional circumstances: and that was what he was doing here. Finally he managed to run the Major to ground: 'Would you kindly make it possible for me to arrange a court martial, in accordance with the terms of my order!' In fact, he could just as well have done it himself. He enjoyed the full backing of the army. But among his peers, he took care always to observe the formalities.

The Major, who all along had been hopelessly unequal to the situation, suddenly saw the funny side of it: 'Any of the officers who are assembled here are as of this moment under your command!' He looked at the Colonel like a clown looking into a mirror. Waited for the grin that was bound to come. Unexpectedly, there was no grin.

'Are these officers disposable, then?' came the surprised question.

'Every bit!' Even an acting C-in-C has some gallows humour. If the clown from HQ wanted to put on his three-ring circus – well, be my guest! The words 'acting C-in-C' affected the Major like nitrous oxide anyway. Who cares, he thought, gurgling to himself. Let these deserters sit in judgement over those other ones! He felt like a hero in underclothes. 'Take anyone you want,' he offered, magnanimously. He had to laugh. His Adjutant appeared behind him:

'Divisional HQ on the phone!'

Just in time. The Major disappeared, before the Colonel could launch into any explanations.

The Colonel surveyed the room. He had always hated disorder. In order to feel in charge, he needed an appropriate setting. That table to the middle of the room. Those boxes out. The floor could do with a sweep. Shame that you couldn't press a broom into an officer's hands. He selected a couple from among those present. The others vanished in no time. The room was suddenly empty.

'What's all that noise outside?' he asked. 'I had to battle my way through here. There was no respect for my rank!'

'Retreat in progress, Colonel!' Now they knew he was a loon. They smiled acidly. That was all they needed. The ground was burning under their feet. But careful, this man was dangerous. He gave every impression of not being afraid. Their eyes met in agreement. They didn't really have the foggiest what his game was. A deserter? You could find thousands of them here! Either the order from High Command was three days old, or the man was hiding something from them.

The Colonel wasn't hiding anything from them. Orders were orders, whether they were ambiguous or not. As far as he was concerned, with the moment he had set foot in the local headquarters, an official process had begun. Now everything would go by the book. By the letter. First of all, the regulations. He was like an old spinster, detached from reality, browsing through old love letters. Reaching down into his briefcase, opening the rulebook. Even the frowsty smell here reminded him of the smell of Courtroom Number Three.

'The list of prisoners, if you please.' He turned to the NCO of the Military Police, who was leaping about like a well-trained hunting dog.

His hidebound officiousness drove the two officers to despair. The Cavalry Captain had a car parked outside. He had only popped in to pick up an alibi. From his place by the window, he watched his driver, who was shifting uneasily about on his seat. Any second, the man was capable of driving off without him. He tried to give him a discreet signal. An inquiring glance from the Colonel pinned him down. The signal turned into an idle drumming of his fingers on the window sill.

It seemed to the Colonel that he had known more dignified assessors in the past: 'May I have your names, please?'

They stammered like schoolboys. Now they were stuck in the local HQ, any hope they might have had of sneaking off was dashed. Feverishly, they looked for an escape. The hammering of the machine-gun outside drove them on. But every idea they might have had failed faced with the unflappable calm of the Colonel. He was just now establishing the name of the soldier, after which the word deserter had been written. He had a vague memory of the episode. The preliminary investigation had already been concluded. The case wouldn't go on for long. Part of him was already thinking about another case, which concerned a half-starved child soldier. In the course of that preliminary investigation, he had formed the impression that the boy had given himself up for lost. Some pathetic story that he'd done it for his mother's sake. Compassion? Nothing about that in the rulebook.

'Bring in the prisoner!' ordered the Colonel. The NCO went off, and the Colonel began to explain to his coadjutors what their duties were. They looked at him. Behind the pince-nez jammed on to the red-veined nose, his eyes seemed to be too close together. He gave his blessing: he adjured the officers to exercise justice, regardless of personal feelings they might have. He himself would preside, and be the prosecutor. The Cavalry Captain with the getaway car outside was engaged as the defence. The other was to be the witness. They lowered their heads in acceptance of their lot. The bare room felt like an execution site.

Bullets were whistling in Emga. Either the Russians were already there, or the Military Police were getting jumpy.

The Colonel was still reading, it was as though he was regaling them with the Christmas story. The defence had to stick to questions of fact. Where there was no factual basis for a plea, no intervention was possible. The witness should attend to the correctness of the procedure. At the end, he would have to confirm that the trial had been properly conducted. And the sentence was his own personal prerogative. Punishment detail was the likely outcome. And he wanted to do a quick job. The two others exchanged a glance: who would have thought it possible!

The driver outside the window had spotted his battery commander, and was banging on the broken window.

'Tell him to get lost,' said Justice. The Captain made a vague and helpless gesture. The man wouldn't be put off. He walked up and down outside the window. He had known his boss for long enough to guess that some sort of higher force was in play here. His manner was like that of a policeman patrolling the street outside a third-class restaurant. Each time he passed, he threw a glance inside. Distracted, the Colonel began to stumble over some of his lines.

'What does he want?'

'I've never seen him before,' lied the Captain. In the gloomy light, his blush remained unnoticed. Finally, the NCO came up with the victim. The two coadjutors were alarmed: if he had earned any punishment, he must have already served it. The eyes of the child with the narrow shoulders seemed to transfix them. They seemed to know everything. The Cavalry Captain remembered the episode with his burning vehicles. He had shouted out: 'Torch!' and that was enough to finish him off. At least thirty men in his company had been witnesses to the fact. He saw their staring eyes. They were petrified. But he had only done what they wanted him to do. His command had freed them from the fetters of discipline. They had lit the bundles of straw with the glee of savages, then scattered to the four winds. Anyone wanting to settle old accounts – and there were some old accounts in his company too – just needed to give this story a bit of an airing. And then it would be his turn. That Justice in front of him, he was just slavering for such cases. He knew nothing of fear. Nothing of certain humiliations. The most wretched life is still a present full of promise. Where is the man foolish enough simply to throw it away? At such moments you feel longing: for a crust of bread, a Lord's Prayer, a drink of water. The boy with the dull eyes seemed to stare right through him. Perhaps punishment wasn't the worst thing as far as he was concerned. If God wanted, he might even survive that . . .

The Colonel opened the hearing. 'We have enough evidence,' he said, rather vainly. 'But, if only for the sake of process, why don't you tell us again in your own words what happened. At that morning hour when the attack was due to begin, you were nowhere to be found? Why not?'

If it had been himself behind the parapet, waiting for the

signal, the question might have seemed superfluous. Perhaps the opportunity seemed there, the next man just out of sight. It should have worked. Something got in the way. When he heard them calling his name, it was too late. At that instant, he would have dashed through the hail of bullets with the others, full of dread. A fit of blind bravery could have made a hero of him. Too late. An agent of destiny pushed him over the edge. The cold face with the pince-nez was at once agent and destiny. The ears that went with that face would no longer hear the breaking of his bones.

In Emga, bullets were whistling. The Colonel seemed to think it was rifle practice. If the boy had just a little common sense, he would draw out the proceedings till the Russians were at the door. Almost unconsciously, the Captain looked out of the window to see his driver starting the car. He wanted to draw his pistol, but he didn't know who to shoot at. The Colonel, the fleeing driver, or the skinny kid who was to blame for everything?

'Just a second,' said the Captain, and simply rushed outside. The Colonel had no time to frame a reply.

The Captain ran round the corner: car and driver were both gone, the street was empty in the hot noonday sun. A couple of wounded men were dragging themselves towards the station. A machine gun stuttered at the edge of the town. Slowly, as though he had only gone out for some air, he turned and went back inside. He walked down the corridor with its whitewashed walls. Past crates full of papers and forms. He stopped for a moment to prop his back against the tall Dutch stove. When he re-entered the room, the Colonel seemed only dimly aware of the fact. In a theatrically raised voice, he was hectoring the boy:

'Do you know what you are? A repulsive offshoot of your mother!' There followed a stream of abuse, and cold sneers. The soldier's face crumpled. He muttered meaningless words, raised his hands beseechingly. He directed his deepset eyes towards the two other members of the tribunal. 'Your mother will be ashamed!' the Colonel went on. 'You coward!'

The Captain winced.

'Tell him what he deserves,' the Colonel turned to the other two. 'Tell him,' he said again, when he got no answer. They both lowered their eyes. The unworthy scene choked their throats.

'Let him go,' the Captain suddenly said, on an impulse. He didn't know where he'd got the courage from.

The Colonel's face contorted itself: 'Is that the word of an officer?' He seemed to be looking about him for a weapon, to castigate his opponent. 'I pass the sentence here!' His voice calmed down. Cool and impersonal. A cold glance brushed the boy. The two coadjutors heard only the conclusion: '. . . to death by shooting!' They froze, as though it had been a judgement on them. The boy stood, impassively. 'And you will carry out the sentence!' the Colonel finished. His hand pointed at the Captain. 'Right now!' The Captain turned pale.

'Me?'

'Yes, you! Behind the building, anywhere you like. There's plenty of room.' The Colonel acted as though the condemned man were no longer present. 'I take it you have at least got a pistol?' he asked coldly.

'I object.'

'Objection declined.' The Colonel looked around. But he had forgotten he had no audience here. He shuffled together the papers with the various rules and regulations. He nodded to the NCO. A pause. The Colonel got up behind the table. Like a bored onlooker, he turned to face the window. The machine gun was clattering away in the distance. The window jingled. A hole appeared in a pane. A fine hissing sound. The Colonel put his hand up to his face. In alarm, he let it drop. It was red with blood. The two officers saw a mutilated face. Red eyes in a gory mask. The shattered pince-nez. The Colonel crumpled back on his chair. Gurgled. Drool trickled from his nostrils. The bullet had shaved away his lower jaw. He had spoken his last sentence.

Unmoved, the Captain let him fall to the floor. Only the NCO jumped forward to try to give assistance. The young soldier still stood where he had been, as though nailed to the spot. The machine gun was banging away at the edge of the village.

The local commandant turned up in the doorway with a couple of men.

'A stray bullet,' said the Captain.

The fat Major shook his head. 'Take him out,' he ordered the soldiers. The NCO, ever helpful, opened the door. 'And the judgement?' asked the Major. He surveyed the young lad. 'That's the wrong prisoner,' he then said with irritation. 'I always knew that Colonel was a fool. If the army wants to make an example of someone, you don't start with privates.' He said: 'You have to do everything yourself! Half an hour ago, I reported back to HQ, saying the Sergeant had been shot. As an example and a deterrent. Broadcast everywhere. And now this idiot takes on the wrong case.' He raised his hand in fury. 'Go on, get lost!' he shouted at the young lad, who – as though waking from a dream – staggered off. 'Get

out!' he said to the NCO. And when they were left by themselves, he looked at the Captain: 'We're over the worst. A
fresh regiment is digging in on the edge of town. They should
be able to hold the line!' His paunch spun round to go, but
then he turned once more to the Captain. He said softly: 'I
want you discreetly to shoot the Sergeant.'

A spider's web trembled in the draught that came through
the door. The firing at the edge of town grew heavier. Two
tanks clattered past the window. On the square outside, a
company of infantry lined up in battle order.

12

The pain was burning in Zostchenko's hip. The foxhole was like a grave. Mistily he saw the tallow light and dark shadows on the walls. Shadows all around. Feverish heat on his skin. He begged for water, and got no answer. One of the enemy soldiers passed him a tin cup: a drop that hissed away on the fire. His throat was rattling. He listened to his breathing: a gurgle. All the wounded were gurgling. Air, air! Surely the grave had to open some time. He rolled on to his side, but that didn't help.

'Tovarich?' he asked into the dark. Nothing. The enemy soldiers didn't understand him. The light burned more dimly. The shadows on the walls started to reach towards him. Beads of sweat stood out on his brow. He reached into the filth on which he lay, groped into bloody filth, but the filth at least was cool. That eased the pain. His hand dug itself deeper. He clawed at the wet earth, brushed his lips with his damp fingers. With one hand he stroked his wound. His hip felt dead. Beside him lay a shadow that wasn't sweating. He found an inert hand in the dark. Pulled it towards his brow. The hand didn't move. It was cold. Suddenly, he flung it from him with disgust. Fever gripped him harder. The grave was warm. He wanted it cold. The light was dark. He wanted it bright. He gurgled. The shadows in the tomb gurgled with him. Fever came with a white rush. Washed over him. The candle flickered. He felt liquid on his lips, in his throat. He thought he could hear a hissing on his hot gums. A hand brushed against his forehead.

'Have we got control of the heights?'

The enemy soldier didn't understand what he was saying . . .

'The heights are strategically important,' said Zostchenko. 'The General himself said so. The General knows everything. There are too many soldiers, and not enough heights.' 'I'll give you the heights,' said a shadow. 'Thank you.' He took the heights in his two hands, and carried them to the General. 'A hero, a hero!' exclaimed the General. He stood in a steel cage. His voice came out of the cage. It sounded hollow, but it could be heard all over. Around the cage was a protective wall of soldiers. He felt his way carefully through them. He had to be careful of the heights in his hands. The soldiers were bleeding from many wounds. 'Set down the heights, and stand with your back in front of the hole, so that your body shields me when I take control of the heights,' commanded the General. He obeyed. The General quickly opened the hole, took the heights, and slipped back into the cage. 'You are a hero, and I need heroes in the wall of soldiers around me,' said the General. He obeyed. The enemy charged. 'Be loyal and die,' boomed the voice from the cage. The soldiers were loyal, and died. The human wall weakened. 'I will come to your aid,' said the General. But the cage did not open. 'May we live?' asked the

soldiers. 'No,' answered the General, 'you must never break your oath.' There was hand-to-hand fighting between the soldiers and the enemy. 'No one is to surrender,' came an angry voice from the cage. He received a blow. Saw blood flowing from a wound. 'Let me into the cage,' he implored the General. 'Back you go!' shouted the General. He was afraid of the General. He fought on, but his strength was ebbing away. The enemy broke into the wall of soldiers. The soldiers fell. The enemy came ever closer to the cage. He was swimming in blood. Blood mixed with a stream of tears. An army of children was weeping for the soldiers. The General in his cage covered his ears. 'Is everyone dead now?' asked the General. 'I'm still alive,' he admitted. 'Fight till you die,' commanded the General. Zostchenko crawled among the bodies of the dead soldiers, and didn't answer when the General asked his question a second time. The enemy knocked on the cage. 'I surrender,' said the General cheerfully. He saw him step outside. The General was sweating, because it was hot in the cage. The General left the heights behind. He had forgotten all about them . . .

Zostchenko couldn't breathe, and he opened his eyes. There were now two tallow lights burning in the tomb. One of the shadows had been pulled into the light. They started to strip him. His face was in the dark. He was whimpering with pain. They cut his tunic from him. It was stiff with filth. His hairy chest was exposed in the candlelight. In his shoulder was a sharp metal splinter. They tugged it out. The shadow roared with pain. A wave of blood broke through the open wound. Then it became unbelievably quiet. Zostchenko could hear the whisper of the burning candle . . .

He had bolted the door from inside. The barracks was asleep. Only the sentry was still patrolling up and down the corridor. Light brushed over the icon. A spider crawled over the wall. The hundred lights of the cathedral were reflected in the window panes. They were showing a new film in the nave. Now the spider was sitting on the icon. It looked as though she was admiring the wonder of glass and gold. The red and green pansy-coloured pearls. The mysterious cross, that was like the marking on the spider's back. It pulled in its legs. Remained motionless. He knelt down, in the way he'd been taught to do as a child. 'Lord, give me a sign,' he prayed, 'just a tiny sign to indicate that You are really there. There is mystery and infinity around You. Show me, make something happen. Forgive me for my doubts.' He folded his hands, and looked down at them. His hands looked unfamiliar to him. There was no sign. The icon did not move. The candles slowly burned down. The sentry paced slowly along the corridor. He looked to check the bolt on the door. The bolt was firm. He had nothing to fear. When the knock came, his heart stopped. He didn't dare to budge. Knelt down, as though crippled. 'Why won't you answer?' asked the voice – it was the voice of the Commissar, not the sentry! 'I can see a light in there, what are you doing with candles? Is there something the matter with the electricity supply?' The Commissar rattled the door handle. 'Let there be a miracle now,' he prayed. He glanced around the room. He was looking for a place to hide the icon. It was hopeless. The cupboard didn't have a door. The pallet bed was too high over the ground. Four bare walls. No hiding place for God. The rancid smell of tallow hung in the air. The electric bulb in its rusty socket hung implacably down into the room. The Commissar was knocking loudly. He had to open. When he got up, his joints cracked. He pushed back the bolt. The door leapt open. 'Oh,' exclaimed the Commissar in surprise, 'an icon.' Candle flames played over his leather coat. He was waiting for a collision of two worlds. 'An icon,' repeated the Commissar in disbelief, and quietly pulled the door shut behind him. It was as though they were sharing the secret together. The Commissar pushed the cap back on his head. 'May I touch it?' he asked. He didn't understand what was happening. He was expecting abuse and mockery. 'We had one of those too,' said the Commissar in a voice full of awe, and tenderly he stroked the picture. 'I – it's only because it's a work of art,' he stammered. 'It's more than that.' The Commissar's peaked cap threw a huge shadow on the wall. The spider drew itself together for an attack, and dropped like a pebble to the floor. The Commissar stroked the icon. He crushed the insect under his toecap. 'Where are your parents living, Comrade?' 'They're both dead.' 'A memory, eh?' The Commissar was referring to the icon. 'I've had it for twelve years,' he admitted. 'Twelve years ago, I was in China.' The Commissar began to reminisce: 'In China, they worship idols!' The Commissar puffed out his cheeks, as if to show what an idol looked like. He had to smile. 'Don't laugh! Do you know what he looks like?' 'He? Who?' 'God.' 'I – I don't believe in God.' 'But you're afraid of him.' 'No – definitely no,' he tried to deny. 'Damned bloody fear,' said the Commissar, and hung the icon back on the wall, turned the light on, blew out the candles. They were standing in the light of the bare electric bulb. The atmosphere of warmth and home was gone. 'Sometimes it grips us, and we don't know why,' said the Commissar, a little pompously. He wiped his brow, as though he had just emerged from a boiler-room. 'You can keep it there. There's no rules against it.' He tried frantically to ward him off: 'Honestly, it doesn't mean anything to me. I told you I just keep it because it's valuable. Like a gold ring, or something.' He stalled. Looked up at the icon. In the electric light, he saw what an inferior piece of work it was. Worthless glass beads. Kitschy face. His attitude to the icon began to change. To see it hanging there on the whitewashed wall, it was just the imitation of a superstition. He felt offended. 'What's on your mind?' asked the Commissar. Then he walked up to the wall, took the icon down, started to turn it over in his hands undecidedly. The Commissar stalked across the room thoughtfully. He felt warned by his cunning smile. He said: 'It's nothing but a form of propaganda.' 'Quite so,' affirmed the Commissar. He went up to the window, and opened it in the very instant that the cathedral lights went out. 'I'm not going to subject myself to its influence any more,' he said. Took the icon, and threw it out of the window. It plummeted down like a shot bird, smacked down on the barracks yard, and broke in pieces. He took a step back, and looked at the Commissar: 'Satisfied?' The Commissar responded: 'I am – but what about God?' In his leather coat, the Commissar looked like a bronze statue. 'His icons are up there,' and he pointed out of the window, up at the stars. 'You're more dangerous than I suspected,' said the Commissar furiously, and banged the door shut after him, plaster dust trickled on to the floor . . .

A hand reached into his face. A shell burst had knocked over the candles. A shadow was feeling its way among the wounded. Another shadow began to sing in the dark.

'Quiet!' ordered Zostchenko. He unzipped his flies, and urinated. He felt the warm liquid spreading between his legs. What a blessing, to be relieved of the pressure. Gradually, his urine cooled. Zostchenko was lying in his own excrement. A layer of vapour hung over his belly. The acrid smell itched his face.

Just as unappetizing was the kitten as she crawled out of her mother's belly in a caul of slime. He had flung it through the air, and smashed it against the wall. (Or was he thinking of the icon?)

The frail little skull shattered like an egg. Blood had soiled his hand. The old cat began to yowl piteously. She trailed after him, along the village street, to his quarters. He looked for a stone, but could only find a long stick. He waved it at her threateningly. She sat on the street, with hair on end, snarled at him like a street dog. He turned and walked on. She followed him at a safe distance. Out of the corner of his eye, he looked back at her, suddenly spun round and charged at her. She retreated on all fours, green eyes fixed on his stick. He had never seen that before, a cat running backwards. The distance diminished. Now. The stick flew through the air, missed her head, struck the cat on the tail. A high-pitched wail. The beast was pinned to the spot. Her back arched like a Cossack sabre. The slime of her young that she had licked off it still clinging to her whiskers. She was unspeakably disgusting. He couldn't bring himself to strangle her. But it cost him something to turn his back on her. Maybe she would jump on him, drive her claws into his neck. He walked faster. Trotted, ran. In panic, he looked round. The cat was running after him. Out of breath, he reached his quarters. Slammed the door. After a gulp of vodka, he felt better. He stared out on the street from his dark room. The cat was sitting in the dirt, not taking her eyes off the door. He reached for his rifle. Devil knows why, but he couldn't get the animal in his sights! Also he was bothered by the window glass. He didn't dare open the window for fear she might leap in. He stood a chair on the table, rested the rifle barrel between the seat and back. Now he got a fix on the cat's head. (Or was it the icon?) The beast was sitting in the dirt, motionless, yowling. He could see her little teeth flashing. He squeezed the trigger and fired. The window shattered, the cat flew up into the air. Turned over. Lay there motionless. He felt profound satisfaction. Then he saw the animal getting to its feet again. The cat reeled, stared at the smashed window. Screamed. Eerily loud, like a child's death screams. She trailed around in circles. He had to shoot free-handed. Bullet after bullet lashed into the road. But he didn't hit her. (He didn't hit the icon.) A dog came bounding out from next door. With tongue hanging out. He stopped shooting. Still the dog stayed at some distance from the cat. It was scared. Slithered about on its butt, restlessly. As though tormented by worms. His hands were damp with sweat. He reached for the bottle of vodka. The alcohol was going to his brain. Suddenly he thought it was all wonderful. The cat in its agony, the dog in its fear. He reached for his bayonet, and ran out. He stabbed at the cat till it no longer moved. He felt like giving it to the dog as well, but he had slunk away, yowling. He looked happily at his handiwork. Cat's blood on his uniform. Red Guards had assembled round him and his victim. In spite of his drunkenness, he could sense their revulsion. He laughed, laughed loud at the sky.

The soldiers in the foxhole were up to something. They shone a light in Zostchenko's face. They pretended they had lost one of their men. He had got used to the stench of his urine by now. His trousers clung to his thighs. It was more bearable when he squeezed his thighs together. He was dozing away. The soldiers' voices tore him out of his doze. He couldn't understand what they were saying. He only sensed that they meant him. The disgust with which they grabbed hold of him betrayed their intentions. They dragged him through the passage. Fresh pains ran through his hip. He tried desperately to clutch on to the damp earth. They tore him loose. For them, he was already a cadaver, decomposing.

Daylight struck his ash-grey face. He cursed the sun where he would soon breathe his last. He wanted to return to the tomb, where he felt sheltered. Not die like the cat in the dirt.

Not like the icon on the barracks yard. He felt remorse and self-disgust. If the icon had moved then, his life would have been different. The kitten would have remained alive. He cursed the icon that had failed to give him a signal . . .

13

First, there was a vague sound from the west, that must be an airplane. Then the silver bird appeared directly over the height. It flew a few loops over the shattered blocking position.

Looking into the sun, Lieutenant Trupikov could barely make out the black Maltese crosses on the wings. The doomed band of Germans sent up white flares. He hoped the reconnaissance plane wouldn't see them in the bright sunlight. He pressed himself against the wall of the trench, and followed every movement of the airplane. It seemed to be less interested in the barren hill than the frozen sector of Front by the swamp, where there was suddenly fearful quiet. The tanks pressed themselves into the ground like frightened beasts. Only the Germans, whose defensive hedgehog constituted a barrier between himself and the line of the swamp, exhibited signs of life. They waved canvas sheets that fluttered over their holes. They yelled and fired off shots, as though their noise could be heard by the men in the machine.

The plane circled endlessly, flew lower, and then climbed up into the sky with a yowl of its engines. As it flew towards the skeleton of the pylon and the debris of the tanks on the heights, Trupikov hoped it would turn away. No, the machine was merely snuffling around. It came back.

The Lieutenant had a queasy feeling. At last he understood why the plane refused to go away. A quiet buzzing became audible from the direction of Emga, and grew louder. Then he made out dark points in the sky. The air became a little oppressive. His men behind the line of swamp began to fret. The tanks seemed to lose their heads. Red Guards ran around in confusion like little insects. And then Trupikov heard the ack-ack guns, dull thumps, leaving little puffs of white in the sky. The squadron broke out of formation. The planes approached in single file.

The reconnaissance plane sheered off as though it had nothing to do with the affair. Until a swarm of rockets hissed from its silver body. The rockets fanned out towards the sector behind the swamp. Lieutenant Trupikov felt ashamed of his relief. Now he could make out the objective; not one of the rockets strayed to his position. Like a hawk, the first plane plummeted past the white fleecy clouds of ack-ack, towards the swamp position. It would pull out of its dive directly above his own section of the trench. Hideous siren wailing filled the air. Trupikov was helpless before the flight of the machine. Lamed with fear, he saw the flat cockpit and the raked wings making straight for him. He saw the bomb detach itself from the belly of the dive-bomber, and travel on in the direction of the flight. Now it was the bomb that threw him into panic. It was almost too much to believe that the thing would fly past his trench, and not land among the Germans either, but instead exactly where the rocket had hit the ground a moment ago, in the swamp sector. Earth spun through the air, a hail of mud, and fumes. The wave of the explosion reached the Lieutenant at the same time as the rattle of machine-gun fire. An invisible fist knocked him to the ground. A fresh howl began. The next greedy maw raced towards him. The squealing siren tore at his nerves. Plane after plane tilted down. Delivered its bomb. Behind the swamp, the earth heaved. The limber of a gun sailed aloft like a flying carpet. The gun turret of a tank flipped up in the wind, and floated over the brush. Performed an almost perfect landing.

The Lieutenant saw no men in this hell. They seemed to be extinguished in the fountains of dirt. But the tanks and all those who still survived behind the strip of swamp did not want to pass away quietly. At various points, the light anti-aircraft guns started to bark. A hail of bullets was launched towards the wailing planes. The machine guns on the tanks replied to those on the planes. A grisly spectacle, which the Germans in their trench watched with equal fascination. Lieutenant Trupikov sobbed with fury, as his tank platoon and all hope of rescue was blown up before his eyes. He kept his face pressed to the ground. Till a mighty explosion caused him to look up. With a savage bolt of flame, a mushroom cloud roared into the air. Wet clumps of mud flopped down in the trench. The guns had brought down a diving plane, the last in the line.

The rattling died away. The ack-ack guns barked forlornly after the departing Stukas. Then they too gave it up. The silence oppressed the Lieutenant. In front of him, on the downhill slope, was the jagged piece of trench occupied by the Germans. An aluminium wing as high as a house was jammed in no man's land. From a distance, it looked like some kind of

memorial. Behind it, and behind the swamp line, the landscape was volcanic. Steam squirmed over the ground. Black
oilsmoke curled around crippled steel wreckage. Here and
there, the tube of a gun pointed nakedly and uselessly heav-
enward. A bush was merrily ablaze like a tuft of straw, and
human figures wandered to no end in among the craters. No.
There was no hope of any support from there. The
Lieutenant turned west again. Behind him the heights. The
bleak hill with the steel skeleton and the two demolished
tanks. No longer a victorious storm battalion. No attaining of
the appointed objective. Future plans, deadlines, projections,
all were as irrelevant as the commands that had led them to
this point. The master of the hill was Death. The Germans
and he, Lieutenant Trupikov, and his men – two useless
groups of men, confronted by death. They might have done
better to come to terms, like businesspeople.

The Lieutenant slipped back into the trench. He ignored the
corpse whose outstretched hand smacked against his bootleg.
One question tormented him: how would he and his men get
back? Over the top? The German machine gun would mow
them down. The only way was through the Germans. He owed
his casualties the order for close-quarters combat.

The first bullets whistled over the crust of earth that was
sheltering him. Further afield, the firing was flickering to life
as well. He stepped up to the dugout entrance, unsure what to
do. They carried a Red Guard past him. One of the kids
they'd pulled out of school and shoved in his battalion. A foot
dragged along the wall of the trench. On his face the astonishment of those who die without pain. The Lieutenant
watched as the carriers held him by a hand and a foot apiece.
They swung the body back and forth. Launched it over the

rim of the trench. Now he was lying on the parapet, facing the Germans. A bullet slapped into the earth beside the dead man. The next one hit his helmet, which rolled with a clatter back into the trench. When a further bullet hit the dead boy in the head, the Lieutenant asked himself how that was helping the Germans. He shuddered. The face was no longer a face. The bullets lashed into the body as into the target at a fairground shooting stall. 'Five, six, seven,' he counted them with incredulity. He reached into the trench for a rifle – there were enough lying around. Cautiously, he pushed its muzzle over the rim. The puffs of smoke betrayed the whereabouts of the other. Glinting metal in the pallid afternoon sun had to be a rifle. Behind that, a patch of white: his face. He aimed carefully. But the bullet landed in something green. There's no point, he thought. There's no point in negotiating with them. They're like wild animals. Either you kill them, or they kill you. There's no other way.

The Major leaned against the wall of the trench just as he had come out of the low-lying swamp. Barefoot. With torn-off shoulder-tabs. A gaping tear in his tunic. Hands and face crusted with blood and earth. He was able to shake off the layer of mud like a brittle crust. He gripped his rifle stock, ready to shoot as soon as his inflamed eyes should see a target, to fight, to punch, to throttle. There was only one thing he didn't want: the mosquitoes. Thousands of mosquitoes were buzzing round the trench. A blueish glittering cloud of little bodies, of tiny pricks. Insatiable for blood. A plague against which he was defenceless. They crawled over his neck, flew in his face, got in under his sleeves, settled on his bare feet. Little primordial beasts. They landed on his skin. Their stings darkened with his blood. They sipped and sucked till his flat hand crushed them, and the frail full bodies were splattered. They sacrificed their lives for a few seconds of pleasure. He was left with the itch. The biting pain. The round swellings. A rash over his collar like a scarf, around his wrists, swelling all over his feet. It was worse than a few shells, which would at least have driven them away for a little while. With his tongue, he licked the swellings on his hands. For his feet and neck, he could do nothing.

He had wanted to go to Hell, and by God, he had had his way. Tricked out with everything a sick brain could think of. And worse than putrescence, hopelessness, filth, itching and mosquitoes were his men. They had received him initially like lost souls, greedy and desperate. But slowly his presence had poisoned the air. What tank shells and hissing salvoes of bullets had failed to do – he had done it: the reins were loosening. The men received his commands with a leaden lack of interest. They eyed him suspiciously, as if he were preparing their funerals. It didn't help at all, that he handed the command back to the NCO. The hatred was there. And now he was afraid of them. Or at the least, unsure of them. He, to whom life was a matter of indifference, who had wanted to throw it away on their behalf, now began to love it.

Here, between the rage of the enemy and the hatred of his own men, it appeared to have some value to him. The grief over his dead daughter, the memory of his wife, became somewhat notional to him. In the midst of this cratered landscape there was suddenly nothing more important than himself. In front of him the bombed scene, the Stuka wing, stuck in the earth like a splinter. Behind him the labyrinth of saps, with the cut-off platoon of Russians. Far back, the hill. Lifeless, cold, distant, like another planet. But he still lived: a filthy creature with bare feet, uniform in rags, disfigured hands, sunken cheeks and ashen skin. From all parts of the trench, his face popped up at him, his fever-burning eyes looked at him. A heap of lonely men. They envied one another the crumbled shreds of tobacco in their pockets. A crust of petrified bread. A fistful of bullets, scooped out of the mire. During the Stuka attack on the position behind the swamp, they had briefly made common cause. They had uttered bone-piercing yells. Had waved the shreds they wore over their nakedness. And then the disappointment when the squadron had disappeared over the horizon. As if they had expected more, even just a sign. WE'VE SEEN YOU! HANG ON! WE'RE COMING BACK FOR YOU! But nothing. They were left behind. Abandoned in the limitlessness of the battlefield. Forever in the expectation that, from in front or behind, the brown wave would roll up to them, shouts of hurrah! to accompany the whines of ricochets, the cracks of tank shells, the twittering of mortars. No, not quite yet. An oppressive silence. Accompanied by exhaustion, hunger and mosquitoes. No bandages. No water. And, worst of all, no ammunition. In their excitement, they had failed to notice how their supplies were dwindling. The first to notice were the ammunition carriers, who were running back and forth to the two machine guns.

'Ammunition!' The cry ran along the winding trench, as far as the foxhole. From the foxhole, someone yelled: 'Surrender, for fuck's sake! White flag!' And, as if he'd gone crazy, the man banged off shot after shot. Aimed ferociously. Applauded every hit with a grisly whoop. The NCO swore at him to get him to shut up. His steel helmet bobbed along the trench, came to the Major.

'We'd better take a vote,' said the NCO. He was panting. In him too, the Major identified his own face. 'We must let them vote, Major. No one will follow an order any more. Surrender or break-out. Last chance.' The Major bit into the palm of his hand. The skin felt bumpy. The mosquito poison burned like fire.

The Major took evasive action: 'You're in charge here.'

'OK,' said the NCO. 'Break-out or surrender?' He held his pistol in his hand, directed at the Major. As if he wanted to use it to get the right answer out of all of them.

The Major bit down on his finger. He asked: 'Do you think we could manage to break out?' Blood oozed out of the blisters on his fingertips. He bit harder.

'Yes,' said the NCO. 'Shit on God if we don't.'

The Major shook the blood off his hand: 'Majority decision?'

'That's right.'

'That wasn't an order.'

'Was.' The NCO rammed the mouth of the pistol into the wall of the trench. The opening was full of earth. If he fired it now, the thing would explode in his hand. 'Answer!' he suddenly screamed at the Major. 'Surrender or break-out?'

'I don't count.' Through a gap in the parapet by the shelter, the Major saw the wounded Russian officer lying. They had just thrown him out. He couldn't see the man's face. But he saw one of his hands scraping at the earth.

'You've got to decide,' the NCO pressed him. 'You first. I've got no time to lose. We're shooting off the last of our ammunition.' The Major didn't open his mouth. 'I need you to vote,' the NCO yelled at him.

No time, no ammunition. Break-out or suicide. Surrender

or suicide. Either way worked. The Major bit into the palms of his hands again. An airburst shell blew up above them. 'I'm afraid I must abstain,' said the Major. The wounded Russian rolled off his place. He couldn't see his hand any more. There was no prison for him.

'Goddamnit, Major!' said the NCO. 'Break-out or surrender?'

'Can't I get it into your head that I can't participate in the decision!'

The NCO examined his plugged pistol muzzle. He banged it clear against his left elbow. The earth trickled over the Major's bare feet. It was as though he'd touched him. 'I demand an answer!'

'All right, if you must – surrender!' The Major's teeth dug into his palms again. The pain from the bite this time cut through his whole body. He could no longer feel the burning of the mosquito stings. His bare soles felt icy. The NCO looked at him: his own face looked at him. But with a hate-filled expression. He had a sense of how the NCO would see him: no epaulettes, barefooted, with the rip in his tunic, grimed hands, and bloodied welts along his wrists and neck.

'Coward!' The NCO turned away.

The word didn't upset the Major. If it wasn't that he'd lately kissed his life goodbye, he would have felt proud. He began to think how to go about it. He didn't have a pistol. What if he took a wire, and stuck the rifle in his mouth? The Russians stopped shooting in the saps. It was almost quiet. The NCO was talking to the nearest sentry.

'Break-out or prison camp?'

'What did the Major choose?' asked the sentry.

'Break-out.'

'OK. Break-out it is then,' said the man.

That's not true, I didn't, the Major wanted to call out. He couldn't make a sound. The NCO's steel helmet moved on. The Major looked for a wire or a bit of string. He found a gun sling. As he loaded his rifle, he thought about how quiet the Russians were being at the former company office. Maybe they'd shot off all their ammunition as well. Maybe he should have voted for break-out. The idea that he might kill himself just before a decisive turn in events gave him pause. His hand shook as he looped the sling round the trigger guard. He permitted himself no distraction. All that mattered was that he was dead right away. The bullet was to go through the roof of his mouth into the brain. He would feel nothing. He propped the rifle between his legs. Checked whether he could use his big toe to pull the trigger. As he looked at his feet, it crossed his mind that he would leave an extremely unappetizing corpse. A smashed skull and a filthy body. As well that no one would see him. As an officer, incidentally, he was entitled to a coffin. But in fact he'd be lucky if they dug him a hole. Comforting that he wouldn't leave anyone behind, wife or child. He wanted to do it in such a way that he fell face down. All he had to do was lean forward slightly. The mouth of the rifle under his chin looked at him like a dead eye. Suddenly the sound of voices came from the foxhole. He heard his name mentioned. 'If he hadn't come, they'd still be alive now.' He wondered what it was they held against him. 'When the Captain called on us to surrender, there were more of us. He's got five lives on his conscience.' Then the NCO's voice again. A quarrel, evidently. The voices grew louder. 'Equal rights for all! You can't ignore me!' The NCO made some reply he couldn't hear. 'Well, shoot me then, shoot me, why don't you!' the voice screamed again. The NCO: 'Do you think I wouldn't waste a bullet on you?' The other: 'Surrender – whatever the Major says!'

A gunshot whined through the trench. Five plus one make six, thought the Major. The muzzle between his legs stared up at him. He should have stayed in Podrova. He remembered the telephone conversation with Divisional HQ. His command: counter-attack towards the log-road. That was only yesterday, wasn't it? Thirty replacements he had ordered to this position. And the dead driver he'd lost in the Podrova cemetery. Sum total from a single day, on his account. And how many days like that did he have to look back on? He leaned forward over the muzzle, mouth wide open. The cold metal brushed his gums. His toe groped for the trigger. Would he feel something after all?

'Major!'

He jumped, pushed the rifle against the trench wall in confusion. The NCO was standing in front of him.

'All unanimously in favour of break-out!'

The Major gazed at his bare feet. The NCO saw the gun, took in the sling wrapped round the trigger . . .

Lieutenant Trupikov entered the shelter. The German Captain was sitting behind the makeshift table, with his hands on it.

'Still no signs of a surrender, Lieutenant?'

He tried to put on a concerned expression. Not a syllable about the air attack.

'No! They're not surrendering!' Another one of those animals, thought the Lieutenant. Here in his cage he behaves like a human being, but put a rifle in his hands and he'll start

shooting corpses. What's he doing here? The wolf with his
sheep's face. Aren't there enough hills in his own country?
I've even seen them myself, green trees, streams, trim vil-
lages. No rubbish or muck on their roads. Ears of corn stand
upright in the fields like soldiers. But they want to take our
marshy forests off us, our dried-out steppes, a few wooden
huts . . . The Lieutenant became incoherent with rage, adrift
on a flood of misunderstandings. He would shoot this
German. That was the obvious solution. A shot in the neck.
He wouldn't have to see his face any more. With the head
bent, it's not possible to miss the spine. No chance of hearing
a cry of pain from the victim. Even before death, the nervous
connections to the vocal cords are broken. An ideal type of
execution. He looked at his victim. Very short neck, he finally
concluded. Curious, the ways in which one can assess someone's neck. Only the German's high shirt-collar bothered
him. Maybe he could get him to take off the tunic first.
But no: he had to shoot him outside. He would have to
take account of the tunic. Then what if the pistol failed? He
could give the command to the Sergeant. He sent him a
piercing look. Why couldn't the man read minds! Suddenly
he ordered: 'In half an hour we're going to overrun the
German position! Signal for the attack will be a red flare.
Every platoon to take its own wounded forward. I want all
units informed!'

'Signal for the attack: red flare. Take the wounded with us,'
repeated the Sergeant.

The Lieutenant gestured towards the German. Surely to
God that was clear enough. But the Sergeant ran out. The
opportunity had passed. 'Let's try again.' The Lieutenant
made an effort to speak distinctly.

'What?' asked the German.

'In half an hour it'll all be over!'

'What will?' the German asked again.

Then we'll leap at each other's throats, thought the Lieutenant. He said: 'Our tanks will smoke them out with flame-throwers. Come on, after all these are your men we're talking about.'

'I've thought about it some more,' replied the German. 'It's wrong for me to do it.' He was speaking slowly and distinctly, the way you speak to a dog if you're not sure whether it'll bite you or be harmless.

'Why not?' All he wanted was to get the German outside, with his back to him, and his neck within reach. His refusal upset his plan.

'Why not? You did it before!'

The German shook his head: 'Do you know who they've got with them?'

'No!'

'Their commander!'

'And?'

'The single soldier who made his way through your lines is my Major!'

The Lieutenant felt a surge of interest in this opponent whom he would see in half an hour. So they've got a few of that sort as well, he thought. A commander who will join his frontline forces during a battle. 'What difference does that make?' he asked crossly. His time was ticking by. Things were coming to a head.

'He warned me,' said the Captain. 'He'll call me to account later.'

So he's just scared, concluded the Lieutenant with relief.

He's scared of his commander. He stared fixedly into the candle flame.

A pit in the woods. Gloomy vegetation, dwarf firs. Pallid twilight behind the treetops. In front of the pit, the prisoners. One next to another. Eyes on the prepared grave. Not a word from their lips, not a word from the group of Red Guards. 'Kneel down!' ordered the Commissar in German. The prisoners pretended not to understand him. Click of a pistol safety catch. One prisoner grinds his teeth together. A crunching, as if his jaw were splintering. A clump of earth eases itself off the wall of the grave, and falls down. Finally, the Commissar goes from one prisoner to the next. Does it with a certainty as if he'd never done anything else. The echo of every shot breaks up in the treetops. The prisoners fall forwards. By the time the last of them falls into the deep, it's night. Just one last dying glimmer of light in the sky. No. It was tempting, but repugnant. And time trickled by. Only a few more minutes, and then at least he wouldn't have to endure any more waiting.

Red Guards carried stretchers into the shelter. The soft groans of the wounded rose from their pallets. Weapons were loaded. The Siberians looped sacks full of hand-grenades round their necks. The shelter, with its smell of carbolic, dirt, and thickening tallow, did all it could to seem homely. He felt a sensation of leave-taking. Taking leave of security. Taking leave of life. With every stretcher they carried out, the apprehension and fear increased. Man after man stepped out into the passage. Hesitantly, with the small, faint hope that it would be the man next to him who would cop it, and not him.

'I'll keep it short,' said Lieutenant Trupikov. 'The situation . . .' He didn't know how to go on. 'For some time we've been cut off . . . A violent break-out . . . our only option. I want you to come with us!'

The Captain looked at him uncomprehendingly. It took a long time for him to understand: 'That's not possible! You said . . . your word of honour!' He was stunned, suddenly cheated of his vision of serenity. Of little barrack huts surrounded by barbed wire . . . no shells . . . no fear of death . . . calm. It was all gone. 'Leave me here,' he begged. 'There's no point. Please understand my position . . .' His stammering seemed to bounce back off the other's stony features. 'I could look after your wounded . . . Sure I could, sure I could . . .' He was talking like a child that hadn't yet learned to lie.

All the while, the shelter was emptying. As if they understood they were now superfluous, the candle flames started to drown in little puddles of tallow. One wick after another hissed out in grease. Only one was still burning, to light him the way to death. On one pallet there was still a bundle of humanity. His breathing was ticking like a clock, but he didn't move. He was forgotten. Like the rickety table, the empty conserve tins, a scrap of bread, the smeared jam, shreds of paper and unusable arms.

'Come on!' ordered the Lieutenant.

The Captain stood up behind the table. 'What about him?' he asked, pointing to the bundle.

The Lieutenant didn't answer. They went out into the passage, the Lieutenant keeping close behind his captive. They pushed aside the oilcloth in the entryway, and emerged into the trench. The bright sun blinded them like a lightning flash.

'Stoi!' ordered the Lieutenant. The Captain froze. He felt the muzzle of a pistol against his back. He turned round in terror: a bottle-shaped explosive lay in the hand of the

Lieutenant. The Russian was fiddling around with a string.

'No!' screamed the German in dismay.

The Lieutenant looked up, a little surprised, the live hand-grenade in his hand. 'You mustn't do that!' the voice yelled in his ear. He stared perplexedly at his hand, and threw the grenade over the parapet where it went off. He had been going to throw it in the shelter. All right, then. He didn't want to be an animal. 'Stay here!' said the Lieutenant. He pointed to the shelter. 'March, in there. Dawai! Dawai!' he yelled, and, almost relieved, walked off along the trench. They moved away from one another, two points on an endless grey plane. The Russian with the short hard stride of a firing squad, bound for an execution.

A red flare rose into the sky over the Russian-held saps. Green steel helmets and brown forms spilled out of the trenches. The NCO jerked the whistle to his lips. Noise on both sides. Whistling rifle shots.

'Let them come nearer!' shouted the NCO. The firing ceased. Only a Russian machine gun was still hammering through no man's land. Then it too fell silent. The Major laid his rifle on the parapet, the NCO shoved his last magazine into his pistol. They leaned side by side against the earth wall.

At the head of the Russians ran an officer. With arms upraised, as though to show his men the way. Behind him stumbled stretcher-bearers with a stretcher. They came closer. Still no shot from the trench. Worried by the strange silence, they fell back a little behind the officer. Took a sudden right turn. The officer ran on. His men veered off into no man's land.

'They're not obeying him!' yelled the NCO.

The wave of the enemy turned into a long column, picking their way over the open ground. Ahead ran the riflemen with their guns, stooped, faces down towards the trench. The machine-gun crew were dragging a tripod with them. And at the end the stretchers. The stretcher-bearers stumbled and fell, picked themselves up again. Their loads swayed. Only the officer charged on ahead. Without a look back.

'Don't shoot!' ordered the Major. 'Don't shoot!' the order went along the line. They watched the men running across the top, and the officer running at their head. He emerged with ever greater clarity, while the others turned into blurred brown shapes in the distance. They could make out the steel helmet, then the grey revolver barrel, and finally the contorted face. He was running towards the foxhole. Two engineers scurried to the place where he would enter their line. He loomed up above the parapet. Gigantic. A broad chest. An unfamiliar being, as from another world. He leaped down into the trench with extended arms. Dull thumps of gunstocks. A gurgle. Then silence. The ghostly queue of men in the distance for a while longer. They melted away among the craters. The NCO and the Major looked at each other.

'Do you understand that?'

'A miracle,' said the Major. They couldn't believe their eyes.

'We can make it back!' the NCO finally managed to blurt out. 'We can make it back!' He seized the Major's hand, and shook it. Laughing, they patted each other on the back. Their grey faces, their dulled eyes, came to life. They slurred their speech like drunks. The rifle with the sling looped around the trigger-guard slipped down from the parapet. Behind them, in the trench, voices began to sound. A tear trickled down the Major's cheek, like a brook through barren earth. Filthy figures pressed up to them, surrounded the Major. A cigarette was passed from hand to hand. Bodies were still littered around, and their uniforms still stank of dead bodies. But they seemed to have forgotten that there were still tanks behind the barbed wire. That it was a long way back to what was now the Front. The warren of saps, the path through the brush. The ravaged hill. The marshy forest in the hollow. And somewhere in the impenetrable thickets lurked the enemy . . .

The Major thought about the way back. He walked along the trench. Only realized now where he was. Took it in. A moment ago, in the grip of fear, the trench had been nothing but a rip in the earth. A narrow gulch full of shit, blood and bodies. With the empty saps behind them, clarity returned to him. He took in details. Not just vague outlines. A heap of used cartridges. The clay balls from the rip-cords on grenades, as white as mothballs. The shattered tripod of a machine gun. The cloven steel helmet. A human foot detached from a leg, naked and waxy, like an exhibit in a pedicurist's window. A step further, dangling over the parapet, a head. Curved eyebrows, like a Mongol's carnival mask. The used air-canister from a flame-thrower. At the bend in the line, the stiff arm you had to push aside that came down behind you again like a turnstile. The supple, bouncy ground. The silent stepping over bodies that were only a thin layer of earth away. The curled-up bit of telephone wire. The dead man spread-eagled against the trench, as though crucified. Only the mosquitoes the Major couldn't see any more. Their blueish swarms teetered in the air like veils, stepped off the trench with him, as if he were carrion, there to feed them.

And then the wounded. They came crawling up out of the foxhole. Stammering words. Oozing bandages. Lightless eyes. Imploring gestures. He had to guarantee them that he wouldn't leave them behind. That he would have stretchers made for them. He saw the badly wounded Russian Captain, and he knew he couldn't tell them the truth. That even the healthy ones would be unlikely to reach their own lines alive. That if things got hot, the bearers would have to dump the stretchers in the swamp. He awakened hopes he knew he couldn't fulfil. He lied. Maybe out of compassion, maybe out of cowardice . . .

He gave instructions for departure calmly and thoughtfully. The order of march. The distribution of the remaining ammunition. It wouldn't have made sense to leave these dispositions to the NCO. When they moved out, the sun was like a red disc behind the skeleton of the steel mast. The Major went first. He pulled the corpses aside that had blocked off the saps, and only took in the earthen walls of the trenches. At a wrecked machine-gun nest, they swung to the rear. That dead Russian must mark the spot from where the Captain had addressed them. The Major didn't expect to see him alive any more.

And even when he did see him, propped against the busted tank, pale, motionless, his first thought was that he was dead, and so he walked past him in silence. So many dead men of his acquaintance had looked at him. The Captain was resting in the shade, the Major was dazzled by the sun; it's not nice to look at a dead man. The Major wasn't thinking of punishment or guilt, nor even of what he would do if the Captain was still alive. He only felt sympathy. He thought of the climb ahead of him, the way through the swamp, the pressing feeling of responsibility. His bare feet trembled with fatigue. Thirst tormented him. And a sharp pain in his lung.

The NCO, who was walking directly behind the Major, stared at the Captain as at a miracle. He had been watching the Major. A faint movement on the part of the Captain had caught his attention. He saw who it was. Was startled, baffled, too excited to be able to speak, and so, mechanically, he did what the Major before him had also done. He passed him in silence.

The Captain let the rest of his company file past. A grey column, longer than he had hoped. Familiar faces, etched with hunger and pain. He smiled at them all. He felt like embracing every one of them. His joy on seeing them again was perfectly genuine. He was happy. Stood up straight. Pushed his steel helmet back out of his face. His eyes beamed at them till the last man passed. Not one of them had looked at him. Not a word of recognition. Not a gesture. Even from the bearers, who filed past with the wounded. He felt as though he'd been buried alive.

He had to sit down, and perched on the shot-up caterpillar belt of the tank. His hands were shaking. He had no sensation in his feet. He looked up with vacant eyes. In the evening sun, everything looked blueish red. The steel plates against which he rested. The trench with its walls. The bushes in front of the hill. The men slowly getting smaller as they went away. The cratered hollow. With difficulty, he stood up. Cautiously moved his feet. Inched his way forward. Looked for support from the edges of the saps. Tumbled past the opening to his shelter, regardless. He had forgotten there was still a fellow lying there. He was an outcast. He didn't care about the corpses he stepped over any more either. He didn't understand he was walking over his position for the last time. He walked through silence, till the gurgle of a man pressed against his ear. The gurgle came from a disfigured face. The face went with a blood-covered uniform of a Russian Captain. It took pain to convert these scattered impressions into a single picture.

'Woda,' begged Zostchenko. He sensed there was someone nearby. The Captain looked at him in confusion. 'Water,' he had heard him say. He didn't have so much as a canteen on him.

'Woda,' begged the hand of the Russian, with a tired gesture. The Captain reached for the hand. He had to overcome some repugnance to do so. Two outcasts. Two dying men, comforting one another. Absent-mindedly, he stroked the battered hand.

'Sonia,' whispered Zostchenko.

That too the Captain thought he somehow understood. What the spume-flecked lips said next escaped him. *If you see the icon, give it poison. Always carry the poison with you. You can never tell when you might see the cat.* It struck the Captain almost as a reproach, the fact that he couldn't understand any of it. 'A cigarette,' he thought. They hadn't left him so much as a cigarette. No, there was nothing he could do for the man any more. The gurgling ended. He was not yet dead, and yet already he smelled of corruption. The mosquitoes settled greedily on his lips. The Captain spread his handkerchief over the face.

He staggered onwards, and already had forgotten the man. And the saps that gave him shelter. The path that would have taken him to a destination. Branches slapped him in the face.

Mosquitoes supped at his brow. Indifferently, he trotted
through the brush. There was something ticking in his ear. He
ignored it. In front of him was the lunar landscape climbing to
the heights. A blueish surface, spotted with dark round hol-
lows. Further up, there were figures walking. Some had
frames they were carrying. His men, perhaps. He didn't care.
The ticking was louder now. The figures flew to the horizon
like little dots. Some seemed to leap into a void. The sky took
on the colour of blood. The earth was a deep blue. The
Captain left the protection of the shrubbery. Next to him, a
little stream started up, and stones clattered down the hill. He
reeled as he planted one foot in front of the other. What have
I done, he asked himself. No thoughts, just fragments of
questions broke through his foggy groping forward. A single
notion kept coming back: justice. He wouldn't have been able
to express what he meant by it.

There was a bit of wire on his path. He stumbled over it,
and fell. When he lay on the ground, he had a different per-
spective on the heights. The light was reflected in wavy
valleys. The shell craters formed picturesque volcanoes. There
were mild slopes and little crevices. As far as he could see, he
saw nothing comforting. The trickle of a little puddle was
like a lake to him. The quest for justice led to understanding.
There are different perspectives, he said to himself. As he
picked himself up, he repeated this thought to himself. It
sounded like a theorem or principle. He dimly remembered
that it was quite old already. In his slothfulness, he had not
made any use of it, ever. He ought to try to understand everything. Memories occurred to him. There was much he had
neglected.

He got up, and ran on. Those of the living dots that hadn't

come to an abrupt stop, had now reached the edge of the height. He and some whistling iron shards were the only moving things on the terrain.

An abandoned stretcher lay across his path. It tempted him to sit down on it. To wait and see what would happen. Whether one of the splinters would finally catch up with him. But he saw dried blood on the carrying straps, and he'd had enough of blood. It was better if the bullet caught him from behind. His back was a good target.

He walked ever more slowly. He wanted to have done with fear. Now that he knew enough, he no longer needed to run for his life. A few more years, an extra day – it hardly mattered, either way.

Finally, the bullet came. It didn't hurt. Just a tap on his back. The heights, the shot-up pylon, the red of the evening sky all sank into darkness. He plunged into a crater, face down. Water trickled into his mouth. His last thought was: Is this justice?

14

When the Runner started up out of his sleep, it was night already. The dressing-station seemed deserted. Only from one tent was there the sound of foreign words and drunken laughter. He was cold. His bare feet were frozen. The coat, which stank of disinfectant, only covered his top half. Far in the distance, flares were playing about in the sky. He felt abandoned, and wanted to get up. When he heard tapping steps, he pulled the coat over his face. The steps came closer. Someone stopped next to him. He held his breath. Straight away, he felt the pain at the back of his head come back. There was a burning in his chest. He was afraid. A hand fingered his coat, and peeled it back.

'Zostchenko?' whispered a woman's voice. It sounded like a sob.

He held his breath, and tried not to make a sound. The sobbing went away. Crazy woman, he thought. Up in the sky, the flares beckoned. Since no one was guarding him, he stood up. With difficulty and pain. The foreign sounds in the tent told him what to do. He wanted to go back. Back where they spoke his language. He tottered rather than walked. With every step, spikes drilled into his knees. His breath pounded. He had to take his time. In the blackness, the railway embankment whose course he followed was his only guide. It was like a black wall. His bare foot banged into metal. He jumped, and then remembered the cannon that had to be positioned hereabouts. The danger of being discovered caused him to forget his pain. He wondered whether he should throw away his coat. If he fell into their hands wearing the coat, he was done for. But he didn't have his tunic any more, and it was cold. Perhaps in the Russian coat they wouldn't spot him for an enemy immediately. He had to consider all the possibilities.

The sky began to pale. Now he had to redouble his caution. When he recognized the guns, he felt some relief: at least he was going the right way. He heard footsteps. Once, he saw a little light as well. He crawled along the ground, and had the feeling he would never reach the end of the position. The row of guns was going on for ever. His worry made him foolish. He stood up and ran. Even though he had the salty taste of sweat on his lips, he felt cold shudders of panic across his back. He had felt the same way when he'd had to take messages across the swamp at night.

'Stoi!'

The sentry's call struck him like a blow. His feet stuck to the earth. With a jerk, he moved off. He conquered every obstacle. Shrubbery, barbed wire, a pile of ammunition. He cursed the pallor of the sky and waited for the bullets that must surely come. When he noticed that he had no more strength, he gave himself up to his fate. Mechanically he pitched one foot in front of the other. He walked very slowly. But everything behind him remained quiet, no one was coming after him. At last, he dared to stop and rest. With panting breath, he hunkered down on the ground. His hands trembled. Then a fresh shock: the play of the flares was stopped. Lost, then, hopelessly, irredeemably lost. Suddenly he giggled like a child. He'd forgotten about the embankment. In the lee of the slope, it wasn't surprising that he couldn't see the flares. He crawled stubbornly up it. When he saw the flickering lightnings again, he calmed down. It was like the promise of home after a stormy sea-crossing. With relief, he slithered back down the slope. The wounds on his legs had opened up again. Blood dripped caressingly on his feet. He didn't take the time to see to them. He had the feeling he could hear a stream. Suspiciously, leaking in all directions, he ran on. The water sounds grew louder. A river must cross this path. He wanted to be certain. But then he realized it was no water-rushing, but the stifled murmuring of many men. He listened. He wanted to yell out: German voices! But straight away his suspicion was alerted again. He could be mistaken. Another word he understood! He crept on, doubled over. A bush blocked his view. He pushed the branches aside: a sluggishly moving crowd of men. Tired, swaying figures, talking in his language. He felt miserable. Prisoners. Living dead, disappearing into the darkness.

He decided to stop playing the hunted animal, and bring a bit of method into his escape. First of all, he had to get hold of a weapon. He climbed back up the steep slope. The place where they had thrown him down must be somewhere around here. Also the shelter where they interrogated him couldn't be far. If he managed to surprise a sentry . . .

'Kto a kto!'

The Runner recalled a shout he had once heard. 'Si! Ajo!'
he called back. His coat and the dark made him safe.

'Ajo!' the sentry's voice came back like an echo.

The sentry stood directly above him on the slope.
Instinctively, his hands groped upwards, grabbed two ankles
and pulled, hard. The body above him fell. He sprang aside,
not wanting to roll down the slope with the Russian. All he
cared about was the weapon. He got up the little promontory
where the sentry had stood, and felt all over the ground.
There was no hurry in his movements. He had time. He was
certain he would find a rifle here. And he found it. He
thought, now I have the gun, and the sentry is at my mercy. If
I kill him now, it's murder, because the gun is already in my
possession. If I didn't have it yet, it would be self-defence. As
he inspected the rifle, the sentry came crawling back up the
slope. Silently, oddly enough. Presumably, he had failed to
understand. In the darkness, the Runner could see no more
than an unclear shadow approaching him. He took aim. It
would be a lesson to him. He shot past him. The Russian
started yelling out loud. Let him shout . . .

The Runner turned: the hollow lay before him like a dark
carpet. Lightnings flashed across it. Red and white lights lit
up and went out, and changed places. They reminded him of
station platforms at night. He felt as if he were on a railway
overpass, facing the forest of signals. The yelling sentry
recalled him to reality. They're not going to get me, thought
the Runner.

He looked back over to the sector where the flares were
going up. He noticed that there was part of it that always
remained dark. A gap in the system of signal lights. As if part
of the line were out of commission. That was the part he

made for. Dropping from the ridge into a wilderness of brush. The ground gave way under his feet. He pattered across a thick carpet. A sign that he was nearing the swamp. Among the shrubbery, he thought he recognized the outline of a ruined hut. Then another, squatter, outline. Suddenly he knew what they were: tanks. He had stumbled into an out-post. There must be a sentry standing somewhere in the darkness. A tingling feeling of unease warned him. Cautiously he approached one of the monsters, to wait in its shelter for the sentry to betray his presence by a sound. Leaning against the chill metal, he heard the deep breathing of a sleeping man, coming from inside the colossus. A flap must have been left open. Strange that he could wait here so calmly, his hand on the steel of a weapon whose apparition had always thrown him into panic. He had the feeling he had better do something to the sleeping monster. Like a child out for revenge, he stuffed some earth into the exhaust pipe. He was too enfee-bled to do anything worse. In spite of that, he felt great satisfaction.

In the dim light of a flare, he had his first view of the height from the enemy's point of view. A great formation of earth, leaning menacingly over them. He understood how they could have fought over it so desperately. It wouldn't be long till he reached the front line. Craters gaped in the ground. There was a sweetish corpse smell in the air. His feet sank into the mire. He remembered the coat, and tossed it in a puddle. A few steps further, and he was in the wire entanglements. No sound. His own position was abandoned, the trench, the sap-labyrinth, the machine-gun nests. He clutched his rifle to his chest, and crept forward. Finally, the trench. With the feeling of liberation, he leaped into it. The only men lying around were dead. He was too exhausted to check whether the NCO was among them. He had the feeling he might have suffered in vain – fear, flight, humiliation, wounds, more flight. If the NCO had escaped with his life, he could have saved himself the trouble . . .

He took the coat off a dead man, the tunic and the boots. Tricked out in a complete suit of dead men's clothes, he reeled on his way. To where he guessed the front line was presently.

15

The local Commandant of Emga turned down the flame on his oil lamp and angled the mirror at the empty chair in front of his table. Then he turned to his orderly:

'Bring in the Cavalry officer.'

He looked at the empty chair in the lamplight. Could be an electric chair, he thought. In that case, it would be better to have the victim sitting facing the wall. So that he couldn't see when he pushed the button. He looked down at the list he had on his desk. A spelling mistake leaped to his eye. Because it was in his own hand, he felt ashamed. Hurriedly, he corrected it. If somebody had happened to read that! He squashed a mosquito between his fingers, and sweated.

He had not failed. That pleased him. Commandant in Emga, during a battle. Excitement, anxiety, and a little fear. Well, that would pass. He was growing older, but his ambition was always young. Once the war had been won, he would contrive some way of embellishing the thing. He could hear himself saying: In the space of four hours, the Russians had overrun our Divisional Command. There was no Front.

Incredible confusion. Then the order reaches me from High Command to hold the retreat . . . The details didn't really matter. He would leave out the thing about the jeep commandeered for him, waiting outside. With his dirty handkerchief, he mopped the sweat off his brow. Just then, he looked like a gnome.

When the Captain walked in and sat down on the chair, the Major went straight to the point: 'What's happening with the Sergeant?'

The Captain reflected for a moment: 'Nothing!' Even though he wasn't well acquainted with the local Commandant, he had a feeling this discussion wasn't going to go well.

'I don't think you've quite understood. I gave you an order. When do you intend to carry it out?'

'Never!' Alarmed by his own boldness, the Captain added: 'There is no legally binding judgement in the case!'

A feeble justification. The Major ignored the 'Never!' He said: 'It's a confused case. The legal officer was a nincompoop. The pair of us are responsible for turning it round!'

'Excuse me, Sir, I don't understand!' The lamplight shone in the Captain's eyes. A moth fluttered round the cylinder.

The Commandant embarked on a lengthy explanation: 'The army wanted to make an example. Everything hung in the balance. The intention was to send a dramatic warning to the men. We might face similar confusion tomorrow. It's possible the legal officer hadn't been properly briefed. He was sent to Emga to carry out an execution. Didn't seem to matter whom he took. Only not a common or garden private. Whom was I to choose? You?'

The Captain felt himself turn red. 'So you chose the

Sergeant, and you gave his name to High Command. High Command, in turn, announced that the Sergeant has been shot. And in the meantime, the legal officer condemns the wrong man. The Sergeant is still alive. It's a tragedy without a body!'

'Our duty is to supply the body!' The Captain slid his chair a little to one side. The light from the lamp was getting to be unbearable. Each time the moth bashed its wings against the cylinder, there was a little metallic jingle. 'But that's crazy!' he said.

The Major made a face. 'The man was a deserter. It's an open-and-shut case!' he said.

'We could have found thousands like him.' The Captain thought of his driver. The bastard had left him in it.

The Commandant wrinkled his brow. 'From the reports I have in to date, we have almost four thousand captured or dead. The Sergeant's company, for instance, seems to have vanished. One more or less hardly matters!'

'But that's precisely why it does matter, sir.'

'What do you want? The man is dead, theoretically. His next of kin have been informed. His name has been taken off the list of those entitled to rations. His number has been cancelled. Besides, every company commander will already have read out the order relating to his execution.'

'An unpleasant thing to have to announce,' said the Captain. The cylinder jingled. The moth was evidently dead set on dying.

'And the critical thing in all that was the announcement.'

'What if we give him a chance to desert?'

The Major shook his head. 'How do you propose to do that? If the Sergeant isn't shot, there'll be talk. One day

there'll be an inquest, and I'll have to come up with the body.
As proof, so to speak. Then what do I do?'

'Surely as Commander of fighting troops, you must have
certain possibilities . . .' The Major shook his head. 'I'm not
Commander of fighting troops any more. The breakthrough
has been choked off.' Suddenly he brought his fist down on
the table. He screamed: 'Your suggestion is treasonable!' In
his rage, he swatted one of the many pencils off the table. He
loved pencils with the tenderness of a collector. He gave the
order: 'You're going to shoot him!'

The cylinder jingled. The moth floated down. Once or
twice more, it shrugged its singed wings.

'Give the MP the order!' asked the Captain.

The Major stooped to pick up the pencil and bobbed up
again. 'The MP may refuse. He knows no judgement was
arrived at!' He smiled a saccharine smile: 'There's one principal difference between you and the MP. That man is clean.'
An embarrassing silence ensued. The drone of a mosquito
which had taken the moth's place hovering round the lamp
was the only sound in the room.

'What do you mean?' the Captain asked, a little reluctantly.

'I have proof that your section left its position for no
reason. If I put your name down in a report, you're done for!'

The Captain felt the sweat come out on his brow. He had
made a mistake. Now he remembered. He should have
destroyed the time-chart. From the entries on that, anyone
could see what had happened. The local HQ had a radio.
Every incoming communication was taken down, with the
time it was received. Probably a radio man in his sector had
even broadcast: no contact with the enemy! But that was
when he had withdrawn. In the order book it would say:

Withdrawing under enemy pressure to point X. The fellow had known that all along.

'Well?' asked the Major.

'Do you promise me . . .'

The local Commandant laughed like Father Christmas.

'May I go now?'

'You may. And – come and tell me after it's all over.'

In the passageway that led out to the square, the Captain felt like a diver, walking over dry land with lead plates on his feet. The square lay in darkness. There was a dull grumbling coming from the direction of the Front. The barn loomed up towards him like a great ship. Involuntarily, he slowed his step. In an hour, he would be a murderer. Half an hour, if he was quick about it. It was like a bad play. He was sitting in the box, looking down on the stage. And all at once, he had been given a part. As a spectator, it hadn't looked difficult. But the nearer his entrance came, the more nervous he got. Did he really have to play along? Yes. There was the time-chart. A harmless bit of bumf, a fiendish compact. Even if he got off lightly, he would still be stripped of his rank . . .

The engine of a car hummed in the darkness. Two tiny headlights felt their way across the square. The dipped lights looked like candles flickering in a graveyard on All Souls'. A pair of boots crunched on the gravel. All at once he was standing in front of the locked iron door of the barn. He knocked. The metal echoed like a drum.

'Come on in,' said the MP, as though it were an evening at a club. A storm lantern hung on the wall. It threw distorted shadows across the table. He couldn't have imagined anything bleaker. Spider's webs hung in the air. Straight away, they wrapped themselves about his face. When he wiped them away, he felt a spider on his hand. He shuddered with disgust. Great slabs of plaster had come off the walls. There was rubble underfoot. White patches of wall like the sheets in a morgue, hung up to dry. 'Is it time?' came the conspiratorial whisper of the MP.

The Captain shook his head. He thought, I'm really not being spared anything here. The fellow will remember my face, and that makes a third man who knows about this, apart from me and the Major. Only now did he start to appreciate the monstrousness of it all.

The MP whispered: 'The Commandant told me you would be coming for him.'

'Why are you whispering?' asked the Captain.

'Pst,' the MP put his finger to his lips. 'He's gone,' he pointed up, into the darkness.

'He's gone,' the Captain repeated, first stupidly and then with delight. It was the best thing he had ever heard. He giggled. He had known really all along that it was just a bad joke. The Sergeant was gone. The only possibility he hadn't considered. He laughed aloud: he was an executioner who'd missed the boat. Some way would be found of sorting the thing with the time-chart as well.

The MP hissed: 'Ssh! The Sergeant's sleeping!'

The Captain felt a bucket of cold water had been poured over his head. 'Can't you express yourself a bit more clearly, man,' he blustered.

'He's asleep,' repeated the MP, aggrieved. He moved on to business: 'I wouldn't mind keeping his pistol. And you have to sign a receipt form for him here.'

'A receipt?'

'The regulations say I have to have a receipt if I hand over a prisoner.' The Captain felt a chill down his spine. He dug his fingernails into his palms. Maybe the Major would like to have the ears as proof.

The MP held out a tattered-looking book: 'Sign in here please.'

'Later, later,' said the Captain. What murderer signs his name, and in advance, for God's sake?

The MP grumbled: 'But he's still alive.'

The Captain saw a steep staircase winding up into the darkness. Worn boards, cement dust, a rickety handrail. He thought: I have to go up there. He's sleeping. How can a man sleep when he's about to die?

The MP's voice chimed in: 'It would just be unpleasant later on, when it's dealt with.'

The Captain made no reply. A shot must produce a vast echo in these ancient walls. The muzzle flash would light up the whole building. Maybe the bullet would miss. Then the Sergeant would certainly start yelling. And what if it turned into a tussle? In the fight for survival, a man is capable of anything.

'If I don't have a light, I'm not going to find him in the dark,' he said reproachfully.

'I'll get him for you,' offered the MP.

'No, no. Not if he's asleep . . .'

The MP looked perplexed: 'But we're going to have to wake him!'

The Captain hastily threw in: 'I mean, I'll do it while he's asleep. That's the best thing.'

'You can't do that.'

'Are you saying I'll have to go outside and do it?'

He made no use of the word 'shoot'.

'Yes. Orders from the local Commandant.'

'How does he want that to happen?' blurted the Captain, incredulously. 'What am I going to say to the man?'

'Ssh! Not so loud. I told him he's being released tomorrow. That's what I do with all of them.'

The Captain admired his cool. 'All right, then, you go and get him.' He felt cold sweat on his brow. There was no going back now. The storm lantern's light flickered like a will o' the wisp.

The MP went up the steps. The boards groaned under his feet. The jingle of keys. A cross squeak from the door. In the dark, a spot of loose plaster came off with a crash. The Captain almost jumped out of his skin. He heard indistinct muttering overhead. A second voice. Then some movement. A man sleepily got off his bed. The floor above bounced. Footfall came down the steps. The handrail began to tremble.

'An officer's come to take you away,' the MP was saying. 'Here he is,' he heard suddenly from right next to him, and the Sergeant was standing in front of him. The Captain stared at the white patches on the wall.

'My watch,' he heard the Sergeant say. The MP replied:

'I don't have it.'

'Yes, but it's gone.'

'Don't you get cheeky with me,' barked the MP.

The Captain thought he had never witnessed an uglier scene. He knew who had the watch. The MP's behaviour had been conspicuous all along.

'What about my belt? My pistol?' asked the Sergeant.

'They're staying here,' replied the Captain in a voice he didn't recognize as his own.

'Wouldn't you like to sign now?' The MP held out the tattered book again.

'No. Later. We have to go now.'

The Captain felt relieved to escape the light of the lantern. While the MP opened the iron door, the Sergeant shook his head and said: 'Without a belt!' The Captain thought he was being ridiculous. As they stepped outside, the booming of the Front sounded like the noise from a shunting yard. Red firelight lay over the forests. Their footfall echoed in the darkness.

The Captain suddenly felt in the grip of fear. It seemed to him the Sergeant was deliberately hanging back. In his agitation, he reached for his pistol holster. Opened it. Felt the cold steel, and took the weapon in his hand. He was certain that the Sergeant hadn't observed his movement. In spite of that, his fear didn't leave him, even though he was the stronger, with the weapon in his hand. Then he remembered that the pistol of course would have its safety catch on. You couldn't slip that off in silence. It would give a click. The Sergeant would hear it. A new gulf opened at his feet. Either the Sergeant would know his killer was walking at his side, or else he would certainly make up his mind to flee. Isn't anyone going to come, thought the Captain. He yearned for a voice, a stranger, anyone. Being alone like this with his victim was unendurable. And where should he do it? That question too remained unanswered. The forest was nearby. But he wasn't capable of marching off into the forest alone with the Sergeant. The trees, the undergrowth, the branches hanging spectrally across the path, the night.

'It's time I got back to my company,' said the Sergeant. He was still that half a step behind him. Was that savvy – or simplemindedness? Fear of death makes a man childish. While the Captain was thinking about what to say, the Sergeant asked him a question: 'Where are we going, Captain?'

Unconsciously, the Captain must have been waiting for such a question. In spite of that, it caught him unprepared. Never had he had to come up with a lie so quickly as now. At least, not on such a scale.

'One or two formalities,' he said. He thought even that had given him away.

'I need a record of the time I've been here. Otherwise, my company really would end up believing . . .'

The Sergeant spoke as one entitled to demand.

Just in that moment, the Captain took the catch off the pistol. He surprised himself. He had done it instinctively, while the Sergeant was speaking. He couldn't quite comprehend such cold-bloodedness. Now he had removed the last obstacle in the path of murder. Just a little pressure of the finger . . . But what if he missed? They had crossed the square, and were approaching a building. There was a board in the way. The Captain tripped, and dropped his pistol. It clinked in the darkness against a rock. A miracle that it didn't go off.

'Your weapon,' said the Sergeant.

The Captain didn't answer. He began feverishly searching the ground. Sharp pebbles ripped his palms. Once, he thought he had found it, but it was just a smooth piece of metal.

'Could this be it?' The Sergeant stooped.

At that moment, the Captain felt like screaming. He couldn't go on like this. 'Don't worry,' he muttered. But already the Sergeant was crawling around by his side. Their hands touched. 'Please let me look for it on my own,' begged the Captain.

'Here, I've found it!' The Sergeant got to his feet. The Captain stayed down on the ground, exhausted. He saw the enormous shadow of the Sergeant looming over him. Something choked his chest. This is the end, he thought, and waited for a shot to fall. A fraction of a second, an eternity.

'Here, sir,' said the Sergeant.

What now? wondered the Captain. His legs could no longer hold him upright.

'Captain.'

He reached out into the darkness. Groped for the man's hand, and felt the muzzle of the pistol, pointed at his belly. Catch off. A gentle squeeze, and he would surely die. 'The catch is off,' he wanted to say. When the grip was finally back in his hand, he felt drunk. The square, the building – everything seemed to stagger towards him. He whispered: 'Let's go on a bit.' Here there were huts either side of the road. Black, wind-skewed cabins. The Captain didn't know where they were going.

'Must I expect another punishment?' asked the Sergeant, with unexpected suspicion. He laughed awkwardly. 'There's no knowing what to expect here.'

They passed the huts, and reached an area that was part of the station. A great heap of wood, fuel for the locomotives. The ribs of a burned-out waggon. Somewhere off to the side, water was splashing into a container. The Captain felt himself walking over ballast, stumbling over rails. To his surprise, he heard himself reply:

'I don't want to leave you in the dark any more. Things are looking very bad for you.' He spoke quite calmly. 'It's a matter of your life. The army has called for the ultimate penalty.'

The Sergeant stopped, startled. His breath came hard.

'I thought I was being released back to my company.'

'The MP lied to you.'

'Then that's . . .' stammered the Sergeant. 'No, no . . .'

The Captain felt him trying to come to grips with his shock. 'Get lost!' he suddenly screamed at him. 'Run, man! Run for your life. It's all I can do for you! Maybe you'll find your way to the Russians. Move!'

For an instant there was silence. The Sergeant panted, and then he had settled himself. The Captain saw the shadow, heard the Sergeant's feet on the ballast. He thought about the timetable. The fateful entries. And then he shot. Once, twice, his finger jerked back the trigger. The shots whipped out. The Sergeant screamed softly. By the light of the muzzle flash, he saw him crumple. The Captain continued to pull the trigger. Need, fear, rage, worked in his tendons. An empty click. He had emptied the magazine. With revulsion, he flung the weapon away. Tears streamed down his face. He turned, and staggered away.

'A bath,' he whispered. 'I must take a bath!' he suddenly screamed aloud, and with those words he never returned to reality. To his dying moment, it was said he had lost his mind from shellshock.

EPILOGUE

Three days later, a cold wind from the sea sucked all the warmth out of the forests. The swamps started to steam. Mists hung eerily over the low ground. The mosquitoes were no longer a problem. Autumn was in the air.

A few soldiers were standing in knee-high mist, before an open grave in the cemetery at Podrova. They had looked for their dead, and brought them to the cemetery.

A field-chaplain, who only days before had been preaching in a proper church, was enthusiastically doing the honours. He had come to the Front with fresh troops. In his initial bewilderment at what confronted him, he was still performing duties that, in a matter of weeks, he would leave to a layman. One of these duties was this burial. He laid his stole round his shoulders, fished a little cross out of his breast pocket, and opened his field-bible.

'The Lord be with you,' he began. His attention was divided between the soldiers and the words of Holy Writ. The soldiers' faces reminded him of the colourless stone ornaments that look expressionlessly across graveyards. It wouldn't be easy to touch their hearts.

'For ever and ever, Amen,' he said aloud. He saw a Major who wasn't wearing boots. His feet were wrapped in sacking. White bandages gleamed through the rough brown cloth. He couldn't see the face, as the man was staring into the grave.

'My dear brothers in Christ,' he said. 'This is a sad occasion, on which we turn to God for support. Comrades have been taken from us. The Lord in his wisdom has willed it so.' This was exactly what he had decided he would say in such a situation. 'God is too great,' he went on, 'for us to discern His purpose. He calls, and we must follow. He is wise, and all-knowing. All we can do is to have faith, even though we do not understand!' An NCO who was looking round at the edge of the forest in a bored way, obviously not listening, momentarily distracted him. 'Even though we do not understand!' he said again. Then he remembered what came next. 'You see the sky over our heads, how lofty and exalted it is. You see the clouds above us! What are we by comparison! Modest little beings!' He noticed a soldier with a dispatch case. He was the only one not to wear a new decoration on his chest, as if for some reason he'd been passed over at the award ceremony. 'We must bear our sorrow with humility,' said the padre. 'Not inquire of God why He took one life, and spared another. God is silent and inscrutable. Only when we are returned to the earth of which we are made, will He come to us and say: There will be light! That comfort remains to us . . .'

The Major turned to the NCO: 'I've got to go. My feet. It's damned cold.'

The NCO nodded: 'Lean on me, Major. I'll help you.'

Making as little disturbance as possible, they left. The soldiers let them through. After a few steps, the NCO said:

'Don't think I'm glad to get away. I actually find it rather pleasant. Makes a change. Anyway . . . I secretly hope there's some truth in it.'

'Yes,' said the Major. 'I'd hate to think that was just another trick.'